Malorie Blackman is an ex-computer programmer who now writes full time. The short story 'Child's Play' was first published in *School Tales* (Livewire Books for Teenagers 1990), and her children's picture book *That New Dress* and an early reader *Girl Wonder and The Terrific Twins* are both due to be published in Spring 1991. *Not So Stupid!* is her first published collection.

She lives in London with a Scottish madman.

Malorie Blackman

Not So Stupid!

Incredible short stories

Livewire Books for Teenagers
First published by The Women's Press Limited 1990
A member of the Namara Group
34 Great Sutton Street, London ECIV 0DX

The story 'Child's Play' first appeared in the Livewire Books for
Teenagers collection *School Tales* (1990)

This is a work of fiction and any resemblance to actual persons living
or dead is purely coincidental

British Library Cataloguing in Publication Data
Blackman, Malorie
  Not so stupid!
  I. Title
  823.914 [F]

  ISBN 0-7043-4924-8

Typeset by AKM Associates (UK) Ltd., Southall, London
Printed and bound by BPCC Hazell Books Ltd, Member of
BPCC Ltd, Aylesbury, Bucks, England

To Neil, with love and affection,
Carole Spedding for her encouragement,
and Mum and Wendy, two very good friends

Contents

Skin Tones

Dying was a great disappointment to me. I had expected burning, choking flames and demons and screams of rage and pain. I had *hoped* for soothing bright lights and smiles and flowers; but what I got was Payne's Cemetery. Payne's Cemetery was really two cemeteries divided by a line of solid, majestic oak trees. On one side – my side – were the bodies of the 'People'. On the other side were the bodies of what we called the 'Others'. On my first day dead, when the sun had just set and the evening sky was a suffocating purple-blue, I woke to find myself buried next to Mrs Statson, probably the biggest gossip anywhere, alive or dead. She had been my teacher for more years than I cared to remember so I knew how vicious her tongue could be.

'Well, well, Tricia! So you're dead too,' she said smugly. 'I'm surprised you didn't die before me the way you always carried on. Look who's here everyone.'

Maybe I *was* down below after all.

'Well child,' Mrs Statson urged. 'What happened to you? What did *you* die of?'

'Loneliness Mrs Statson.' I smiled. 'I missed your gossiping tongue so much.'

'Don't get smart with me Tricia.' Mrs Statson frowned. 'You always were no better than you should be.'

'Well you'd know all about that wouldn't you,' I said sweetly. *Eternity next to this woman?! God forgive me my sins!*

'Never mind Mindy Statson. She has the fastest tongue on either side of the oaks.' I looked at the man who had just spoken. I recognised his face although I didn't know his name. He worked . . . or *used* to work . . . in the garden of one of the 'Others'. In fact if memory served, he was quite a famous gardener and constantly sought after in the City. He had a rugged, interesting rather than handsome face and was almost as broad as he was tall and that was saying something.

'Tricia, you have to understand something,' he said. 'The first rule in this place is that we each must tell what brought us here.'

'Why are *you* here?' I questioned. By this time more and more 'People' were gathering around. A few I recognised, most I did not.

'I died of a heart attack,' he said.

'And what is this place?' I asked. 'Heaven? Hell? . . . or somewhere in between?'

'We don't know,' he replied. 'It's not too bad though . . . once you get used to it.'

That could be said for anywhere in the universe.

I looked up at all the faces staring down at me before scrambling to my feet. I don't like to be looked down on.

'Are you in charge here?'

He smiled before replying. 'In charge of what? There's nothing to be in charge of . . .'

'What's your name?'

'Oliver.'

'Hello Oliver.' I held out my hand, which he didn't seem to see.

'We're still waiting to hear how you died,' Julia Greeg piped up from behind him. I never did like that woman. She was responsible for whipping up the mob that killed my best friend Rachael. Rachael believed in live and let live, even when it came to the 'Others' and she'd made a lot of enemies because of those beliefs.

Julia Greeg managed to convince a few drunken hotheads that Rachael was a fraterniser – worse than a murderer in our colony. They went to her home and burned it down whilst Rachael was inside.

'Is Rachael here?' I eagerly looked around the crowd. At least Rachael's presence would make this place bearable. I had hated Payne's Cemetery when I was alive, but now . . .

'No,' Julia said smugly. 'She didn't make it here.'

'She didn't miss much.' I spat back.

I remembered that Julia Greeg had been knocked down and killed by a hit and run driver. Everyone knew that the driver had to be one of the 'Others'. After all, they were the only ones who drove, but no one knew exactly who had killed her. Or if any one *did* know they certainly weren't saying. Not that it would have made much difference, the driver would be tried by his peers, and found not guilty. After all, it was only one of the 'People' who had died and we 'People' didn't matter. My only regret about Julia's death was that I hadn't been the driver.

Julia marched forward and grabbed my arm. 'Tell us how you died. We won't ask you again,' she hissed at me, her cold breath fanning my face.

I looked down at her arm, feeling her bony fingers clutching at my flesh. 'Move it or lose it,' I said quietly. She removed her hand immediately. Julia may be a coward but she's no fool.

'I'm here . . .' I spoke slowly to the eager faces crowding around me, 'I'm here because I killed one of the "Others".' It was the truth but I didn't tell them to get their approval, I just wanted them to leave me alone. Some cheered, some smiled, every hostile expression disappeared. The atmosphere changed immediately. I was accepted. I listened to their eager questions firing at me – questions I wasn't ready to answer.

'Which one . . .?'

'What happened . . .?'

'Which of the "Others" was it . . .?' Maybe this *was* Hell after all . . .

'LEAVE THE GIRL ALONE,' Oliver bellowed suddenly. 'She's only just got here.'

Silence.

'Well, girl, you can't have been all bad if you took out one of the "Others".' Mrs Statson smiled. That was the first time I had ever done something right in her eyes. She belonged to a resistance movement that I considered a waste of time and I had told her as much when I left school. She never forgave me for that when we were alive. I *should* have been a prime candidate . . . My mother – a singer – was taken to the City to perform for the 'Others' when I was only five and we never saw her again, then my father had been killed in a hunt organised by the 'Others' a few years afterwards. But I just wasn't interested.

I walked away from them, towards the edge of the cemetery, ignoring their whispers behind me. I had to get out of this place. Eternity here would drive me crazy. The cemetery was bordered by a low, white, wooden fence which gleamed in the cemetery light.

'It won't work,' Oliver said quietly from behind me.

I ignored him and climbed over the fence, only to find myself back on the cemetery side of it. I tried again and again and again – and got nowhere.

'You're wasting your time,' Oliver smiled sadly. 'I've tried. Hell, I've been here for eight years but still a day doesn't pass when I don't try to get out.'

I turned to look at him. 'So, we're all stuck here . . . birds of a feather.'

'That's about the size of it.'

I looked around. 'What about getting out from the other side of the oaks, past the graves of the "Others"?'

4

'I don't know. Besides, the "Others" would never let you get far enough to find out. But I don't think they can leave any easier than we can. Otherwise they wouldn't still be here either.'

'Does no one ever cross over to their side?'

'Never,' Oliver stated firmly. 'And if you want to stay healthy, I wouldn't try it.'

'What would they do to me? Kill me? In case you hadn't noticed, they've done that already.'

I'd only been here a few weeks, before losing track of time completely. Time was a measure against which I'd nothing to hold. I sometimes glanced over to the side of the 'Others', past the oaks, but I never saw him. I wondered if perhaps he searched for me as I searched for him . . . if he's over there at all. But it's not as if I can ask anyone for information about him. I don't talk to anyone really, except Oliver that is. *They* all want to know every little detail of how and why I killed one of the 'Others', which one I killed, and how I died, and I'm not prepared to open myself up like a book for them to read. They wouldn't like the answers anyway.

One late evening I sat just outside a circle of 'People' discussing the 'Others' – again – but I wasn't really paying attention. The same old boring diatribes that I had heard when I was alive were being aired yet again. But then – of all people – something Julia said caught my attention.

'I'm telling you that there is something very strange about their Zenerths. They say their music is unique – brought from their world – but the Zenerths . . .'

'Don't let your imagination run away with you,' an old man across the circle from her snapped. 'Their music is as disgusting – as depraved – as they are.'

'I never said it wasn't,' Julia snapped back. 'I just said . . .'

'I think the Zenerths produce some of the finest music I have ever heard . . . from anywhere.' Although Oliver's voice was quiet it seemed to carry throughout the whole of our side of the cemetery. Suddenly not a sound could be heard.

'How can you say that?' Mrs Statson demanded angrily. 'The Zenerth is one of *their* instruments. How can you possibly say that it produces fine music?'

Oliver shrugged. 'Because in my opinion it does. Just as I can look at a house burning and admire the form and beauty of the flames but abhor the violence and destruction it causes.'

'Surely one can't be separated from the other?' someone else demanded.

'Why not?' Oliver shrugged again. 'You all know how I feel . . .'

I stared at Oliver but without really seeing him. The arguments flying around me faded to a slight buzzing which could have been inside my head. I was no longer in Payne's Cemetery, no longer dead. Instead I looked back into my past, which was as clear and as vivid as my present which was all I had left.

I could see it, the five-sheet Zenerth taking pride of place on the wall. And he stood below it, proud of its lines, its colours. This was a particularly unusual Zenerth as some of the sheets were square and oval as well as circular. The largest sheet was forty centimetres square, held taut in its wooden frame which overlapped a smaller oval frame, which in turn was held at one edge between two circular oaken frames. Another large oval frame touched all the other frames at some point and formed the base of the instrument. He took it down and started to play it, stroking first this sheet then that one, coaxing the low, sweetly-sad music from three sheets and formless designs from the other two until all the sheets filled the air with lights and colours in a eurhythmic pattern. Then he began to sing to me, accompanied by the Zenerth which he stroked and caressed. I was mesmerised.

'Tricia? Tricia are you all right?'

Dazed, I looked at Oliver. 'Yes. Yes, I think so,' I said, confused.

'Come with me,' he suggested. I stood and followed him to the fence which defined our prison. He sat down with his back against the fence and motioned for me to sit beside him.

'Pete and Julia and Mindy Statson, in fact all of them here are exactly the same.' Oliver sighed, deep contempt in his voice. 'Sometimes I wish I had behaved slightly better or slightly worse when I was alive – anything so that I didn't have to end up here. But you're different. You're not like them, yet. I can see it in your face. You and me, we're more alike . . . kindred spirits . . .'

'Surely you and I are here because we *are* like them,' I replied with sarcasm. It didn't take a genius to work out what was going on, and the 'Others' past the oaks on the other side of the cemetery were probably exactly the same as us. We were two wings on the same bird. Oliver didn't say anything. He just glared at the others milling about aimlessly away from us.

'I killed Brockson–4,' I said suddenly. 'I . . . I murdered him. That's why I died . . .'

'Brockson–4!' Oliver said aghast. 'The colony leader's first born . . .?'

'The one and only. I picked up his gun . . . and shot him dead . . .'

Oliver looked at me. I looked ahead, through the oak trees to where he might be watching me . . . even now. I could feel the curiosity burning through Oliver but he didn't speak and I appreciated that.

'He told me how the Zenerths are made and then he took down the five-sheet Zenerth he kept on the wall and started playing for me.' Still I didn't look at Oliver, my eyes picking through the darkness past the trees. 'You're right, Oliver. The Zenerths do make a very beautiful sound. And I'll tell you why. The sheets are our skin! The skin of "People" . . . talented singers and artists. The "Others" have developed a way of preserving the talent in our skin. It has something to do with the way those chosen for a Zenerth are killed. Each set of "People" is carefully chosen . . . they have to complement each other . . .' Without looking at him I knew I had Oliver's full attention now. 'Brockson–4 told me all about the process. He delighted in telling me how clever the "Others" are. That's why, when *they* play, you can see and hear the lights and sights and sounds of us, the "People" . . .'

At last I turned towards Oliver. He was staring at me, profoundly shocked. 'I suppose I should be grateful,' I said, close to tears. 'I'm here, trapped in this cemetery, but independent still and with a mind of my own. It would be worse if I was trapped inside a Zenerth, waiting on the hand of one of the "Others" to bring me to life. If you can call it life, trapped in a wooden frame waiting to perform for an audience.'

'I don't understand,' Oliver whispered. 'How do they . . .? Where do they . . .?'

'The best and most creative talents are always taken into the City to perform for the "Others", you know that. Only they aren't allowed to perform as themselves . . . they are *transformed*. That's the word Brockson–4 used. You know that once our musicians and artists are selected they're never seen again, and yet it is still considered by some to be an honour to be chosen. Only the top-ranking officials and a few involved in the manufacturing process for the "Others" know the truth. Our musicians and artists don't live in ease in the City . . . they live on in the Zenerths, alive but dead. Perhaps theirs is the true Hell.'

'And that's why you killed Brockson–4?' Oliver asked me quickly.

I bent my head. 'Yes . . . when he started playing his Zenerth for me . . . when he was *so* proud of it . . . something happened to me, inside.'

Oliver didn't wait to hear any more. He jumped up, calling everyone to him. His voice was loud, bellowing. I scrambled to my feet. What I had told him had been for his ears alone. I didn't want it shared but I realised now that I had been mistaken in confiding in him. Helplessly I watched as he told everyone the secret I had told him. There was a hushed silence when he finished, some people stared past the oaks, but most people stared at me.

'Three cheers for Tricia,' Julia shouted. 'Three cheers for the woman brave enough to kill the son-of-slime!'

I clenched my fists behind my back as they cheered me, my nails digging deeply into my palms. Was he over there, watching this?

Julia came to me when the cheering finished. 'Did you get a chance to tell anyone else the truth about the Zenerths? Any of us who are still alive?'

'No,' I said quietly. 'The Brockson security force found me kneeling over Brockson–4's body. They kept me there until his father arrived . . . and then his father . . . his father killed me . . . there and then . . .' I remembered his gun pointing at me; I remembered waiting for the blast to tear into me.

Julia frowned deeply. 'That's a shame. We'll have to find some way of alerting the others of our kind who are still alive to what's going on. There *must* be some way out of here! We have to find it now, to warn them. It's a shame you didn't spread the word before they killed you too.'

'A lot of our artists don't go to the City to perform for the "Others",' I told her. 'They hide out where the "Others" will never find them. Our art won't die out.'

'No thanks to the "Others",' Julia retorted.

'No thanks to the "Others",' I agreed.

I remembered the look of surprise on Brockson-4's face when I shot him. Surprise, then horror, then hatred. I hadn't cared then, I had hated him so much. I hated him for not understanding, for confirming that he was indeed one of the 'Others' and not different, not special as I had always thought . . .

Angry calls and whistles filled the night from our side of the cemetery.

'You bastards . . .'

'Scum . . .'

A line of 'People' stood before the oaks screaming at the 'Others'. The 'Others' were shouting back, just as angry, as filled with hate as us 'People' were. I walked over to our line to stand in the middle and saw Brockson-4 on the other side of the oaks.

So, he still hated me. I was glad. If he hadn't hated me then I wouldn't have seen him again. But then I saw it . . . and shock tore through me like the gun blast that had ripped into my body. Brockson-4 had his Zenerth slung across his body, his hands resting lightly but possessively on the instrument. We stared at each other . . . Brockson-4 looked at his Zenerth, then back at me and his hands fell slowly to his sides.

'Listen to me, listen to me,' I shouted. Gradually the cemetery quietened. 'I killed Brockson because he owned a Zenerth, because he played it in front of me and was proud of it. And then *his* father killed me. I think Brockson and I should finish what we started. A fight to the finish right here, right now. I won't mind going to Hell if I know he's down there with me too.'

'I agree,' Brockson–4 replied slowly.

'Tricia, let me fight for you,' Oliver demanded, stepping forward. From the hatred on his face I could see that Payne's Cemetery was where he belonged, just as we all belonged there whether we admitted it to ourselves or not.

'No Oliver. For once I'm going to stand up for myself. Brockson belongs to me.'

'Just as you belong to me,' Brockson–4 replied. His familiar rasping voice sent a chill down my spine. I could see him clearly; he could see me.

'And where I'm going, I won't need this any more,' Brockson–4 added gravely. We all watched as he walked towards the cemetery fence. He unstrapped the Zenerth, looking down at it for several moments, and I wondered what he was thinking. Once I would have said without hesitation that I knew . . . Suddenly, he threw the instrument over the fence. I watched as it spun further and further away from us. I never saw it hit the ground. My eyes stayed on Brockson–4 as he turned and walked back.

A silence of anticipation settled on both sides of the fence. Brockson–4 moved forward until he stood just over on his side of the line of oaks. I moved to stand opposite him. We were touching-distance apart. He hadn't changed at all. Strange, but somehow I had expected to see some difference in him. I expected his eyes to be colder, harder, but they weren't, they were just as I remembered them. I remembered all the times we had lain in bed together just holding each other. He'd told me he loved me, that we would go away together . . . somewhere where we could find some peace. He'd hire a ship to take us to Trivv which was habitable – but only just – and therefore hadn't yet been colonised. Life would be difficult but at least we would be together, he promised – and that was all either of us cared about. I had packed and gone to his house as I did each morning since I started working there a year before. The guards let me through as usual without checking my holdall. I finally made my way to Brockson–4's bedroom, avoiding more guards along the way, but I had done it so often before that I wasn't anxious.

We sat down, his arm around me as we whispered about our future. 'No second thoughts? No regrets?' Brockson–4 had asked.

'None.' I smiled. 'What about you?'

'None,' he replied.

'Did you get everything we'll need?' I asked eagerly, knowing that even if he said no it wouldn't really matter.

'Most of it is in the ship already, but take this,' he ordered, taking the gun from the table by his bed and pushing it into my hands.

I recoiled from the weapon. 'What's this for?'

'In case we run into any of the guards on our way to the ship. I'll have one as well, but it'll be safer if we both carry one.'

'Do we have to? I mean . . .'

Brockson smiled, hugging me closer to him as he put the gun in my hand.

'Once we're on the ship there'll be no more need of the guns, Tricia. I promise.'

'And no one will follow us?'

'No one will know where we are. And with the Cloaker aboard no one will be able to find us anyway.'

'Does the cloaking device work?' I worried. I felt sure something was going to go wrong.

Brockson–4 just laughed. 'You're never happy unless you've something to worry about. We will be fine. We don't have far to go to get to the ship, the Cloaker *does* work and I love you. So what else matters?'

'Nothing,' I replied, and we kissed. We took one final look around his room, the room where we had first been together. Then Brockson–4 saw his Zenerth, high up on the wall. He smiled eagerly, telling of the nights when he would play for me whilst we were alone on Trivv. I said it would be too dangerous to take it but he insisted, saying that next to me it was the thing he prized the most. Then he told me all about this strange musical instrument and I couldn't understand how he could even profess to love me and yet own such a thing. For the first time I saw him as the alien he really was.

A different perception, a different morality . . .

Looking at Brockson–4's face now I could see that he was remembering too. We'd had so much to look forward to together. Even now I still didn't understand exactly what had happened. How could dreams just disappear so quickly? He had died hating me . . . I had died hating him and both for the same reason.

Brockson–4 grabbed my hands in his and a cry rose from both sides, before the tense silence fell again. I looked at Brockson, waiting . . .

Suddenly he smiled at me.

Sadly I smiled back.

He still loved me, I could see it in his eyes. Just as he could tell by looking at me how I felt about him. He kissed me. Somewhere far away I could hear the oak trees roaring at us but they didn't matter any more. Nothing mattered except us. Brockson *was* a murderer – but so was I. He came from a race of murderers who couldn't see that what they were doing to us was wrong. Maybe Brockson *had* realised exactly what the Zenerth meant to me when he threw his most prized possession away? I didn't care about that any more. We were damned Brockson and I . . . damned to each other. Damned because we loved each other, and nothing could change that now.

When we stopped kissing, we held each other tightly, our eyes closed as we waited for the rest to descend on us and rip us apart. Nothing happened.

'Brockson . . .' I said uncertainly, opening my eyes.

'Come with me.' Brockson smiled. We walked towards the cemetery fence together, our arms linked, our eyes focused only on each other and nothing else. I could hear the roars of fury around me, but they were distant, totally external.

We stepped over the fence and carried on walking.

Dad, Can I Come Home?

'Dad? Dad! It's Eve. How are you? What are you doing with yourself? Are you all right?'

'Eve? Eve darling, how are you? God, it's good to hear your voice. Where are you? Why can't I see you?'

Eve smiled happily. It was so good to hear if not see her Dad again. Somehow it made the idea of returning home seem closer and more real. 'Dad, the screen of this video-phone isn't working. And the fleet's just returned to Tdir-ah so the queues to use the phones are *ginormous*. It was use this phone or wait for another week to find a phone with a working screen.'

'No, no, it's enough just hearing your voice, bunny. Are you all right?'

'I'm fine Dad.' Eve smiled again, stretching out a tentative arm to the blank screen before her. 'I've missed you so much. I just can't wait to get home.'

'So the reports are true? The war *is* finally over?'

'The war's over. The treaty was ratified three days ago. I should be home within the week, if the shuttle bus doesn't give up under the strain.'

'Bunny that's great news. Wait till I tell Joe and Luke, and especially Morgan – eh!'

Eve's cheeks burned. 'Dad, stop teasing! Besides, Morgan is probably married with eight kids by now.'

'Of course he's not married. He's waiting for you. Mind you, if you told him that, he'd laugh in your face but it's the truth.'

'Is it, Dad? Is it really?'

''Course it is.'

'Listen Dad, I can't stay on the phone for much longer. There's a time limit on all comms to Earth until further notice. I . . . I wanted to ask you for a favour though.'

'Go ahead bunny.'

Eve swallowed hard. This was it. 'You've met Janice my co-pilot. Did you like her?'

'Yes of course I did.' Eve heard the surprise in her father's voice. She ran her dry tongue over her lips.

'It's just that . . . well, we were shot down over Zitunm . . .'

'WHAT! You didn't tell me that . . . are you sure you're . . .'

'I'm fine,' Eve interrupted. 'But Janice . . . but Janice isn't, Dad. She was thrown clear but she went back to get me. She saved my life.'

'So what's the matter with her?'

'She . . . she was shot dragging me clear. Shot with a senso-blaster.'

'Oh my God!'

'Exactly. She's lost an arm and both of her legs and her face is severely burnt – almost beyond recognition. And she's not eligible for artificial limbs because she broke the rules by going back for me. I know those artificial limbs aren't much use but at least they're better than the nothing she's going to get because of me.'

'Oh my God. That poor, poor kid. And she was so pretty, so full of life. How's she taking it?'

'Not too well I think.'

Silence.

'Eve? What's the matter bunny?'

'Sorry Dad, I was just thinking.' Eve forced herself to continue, 'Janice smiles a lot but I think that deep down

16

she feels very scared, and very alone. She has no family, no one to go back to. So I said that she could stay with us.'

'Stay with us? For how long?'

'For good.'

Eve listened to the silence that filled the video-phone booth. The unspoken plea reverberating through her mind deafened her.

'Eve darling, maybe Janice can stay for a day or two, or perhaps even a week, but no way can she live with us permanently.'

'Why not?'

'Eve, use your head. I'll always be grateful to Janice for saving your life. Always. But we have to face the facts. Janice is a cripple . . . she'll need a lot of time and attention. She'll require a lot of care, not to mention money. Our home is too small to have her here permanently and it would cost too much to adapt it.'

'But Dad, she saved my life. Couldn't we at least try? She wouldn't be too much trouble . . .'

'Yes she would darling. Don't you think I'd love to say yes but I can't. Maybe she could go into a hospital for the war wounded and we could visit her?. . .'

'She'd hate that. *Please* Dad . . .'

'I'm sorry bunny but the answer is no.'

'But I've already told her she could live with us.'

'Then you'll just have to untell her.'

'Couldn't we just try, Dad. *Please*, for me?'

'No, Eve. She saved your life and I'll always – *always* be grateful for that but she'd be too much of a burden.'

'Burden?' Eve whispered.

'I'm sorry Eve.'

Silence.

'Come on Eve. Let's not argue. I haven't spoken to you in over two years. Tell me all about . . .'

'I can't Dad. My time's up now.'

'Already?'

' 'Fraid so. I'll see you soon. Bye Dad. I love you.'

'I love you too bunny. I'm going to give you such a homecoming. And Eve. I'm sorry about Janice, but you do understand . . .?'

'I understand Dad. Bye.'

'Bye darling. See you soon.'

Eve switched off the video-phone. She stared up at the peeling, dingy grey paint on the ceiling . . . and cried.

'Mr Walker, it's Janice Sonderguard here.'

'Janice? Well, hello Janice. How are you?'

'I'm all right Mr Walker.' Janice studied the image of Eve's father on the phone. He was just as she remembered, his hair grey at his temples but jet everywhere else. A neat, trim moustache and his skin the colour of oak, his body as sturdy as oak. And smiling eyes. A man you instinctively trusted. Solid, dependable. Only he was frowning now.

'Why Janice, Eve told me that you'd lost an arm and your legs. Have the rules been relaxed? Have you received replacements after all?' Janice turned away from the screen, her lips a tight, bitter line. It didn't matter what the politicians and the diplomats said, the war wasn't over . . . not by *any* means.

'Congratulations. Eve must be so pleased for you.'

Janice turned back to the screen, staring at Mr Walker's broad grin.

'Mr Walker, *please*.' Janice hugged her arms around her body before dropping them to her sides. 'Mr Walker, please prepare yourself. I . . . I've got some bad news.'

'Eve,' Mr Walker said immediately. 'What's wrong? Has something happened to Eve?'

'Mr Walker, I don't know how to say this. Eve . . .

Eve committed suicide this morning. I . . . I . . .' The man and woman stared at each other.

'Eve . . .?' Mr Walker whispered. 'She didn't . . . she wouldn't . . . What are you talking about?' The question was shouted at Janice.

'*Please* Mr Walker, I'm telling you the truth. She's dead,' Janice shouted back. 'She's dead,' she whispered.

'But why? WHY? I don't understand.' Janice jumped as Mr Walker punched the screen. 'Why are you doing this to me? Why?'

'Mr Walker, Eve spoke to you last night. Did you see her? What did she talk about?'

'What . . .?' Mr Walker shook his head slowly, utterly bewildered now, utterly lost. 'I can't . . . I . . . never saw her yesterday. The screen in the video-phone booth wasn't working . . . She talked about you, she wanted you to stay with us.'

'Me?' Janice said slowly.

'She told me that you'd lost an arm and both legs.'

'Oh I see,' Janice whispered.

'I don't understand,' Mr Walker pleaded.

'Eve left you a letter. Can I read it to you?'

Mr Walker nodded slowly.

Janice removed the letter from her overall pocket. There was sand in her throat, threatening to choke her as she began to read:

Sorry Dad. I love you. You've explained everything to me very carefully and I think this is the best solution for everyone.

'What does that mean?' Mr Walker interrupted. 'Eve *can't* be dead . . . I don't believe it.'

'Mr Walker, let me show you Eve. She's . . . in the morgue. I can transmit the image to you.'

'I don't understand any of this . . .'

Janice keyed the necessary commands into the console

beside the video-phone and the morgue appeared
without warning, filled to overflowing with row upon
row of body capsules. Janice began to key in the
commands to home in on the appropriate capsule.

'Mr Walker, did Eve tell you about our crash on
Zitunm?'

'Yes, she told me how you saved her life.'

'I didn't save *her* life Mr Walker,' Janice said quietly.
'It was the other way around. She came back for me . . .'

A new image filled the screen now. There in her
capsule lay Eve Walker, Captain of the SAXICON
ship, with no legs and only one arm and a badly scarred,
almost unrecognisable face.

The Ash Bearer

The tall, stately black woman carried the urn of ashes in both hands, her ebony hair curled right down to her shoulders. Her body was covered by coarse beige material like sack cloth; her feet bare. She owned nothing else – just her urn of ashes. As she walked through the village, the villagers all stood back, fear and loathing for the unbidden, the unwelcome, clouding their eyes . . . stiffening their bodies. But they allowed her to pass.

The Ash Bearer held her head high, her eyes looking neither right nor left. Before her the villagers were silent: behind her, they muttered and pointed. Then Luke, the bravest man in the village, moved to stand before her, barring her way, but the Ash Bearer would not go around him and that made Luke angry.

'Who are you? Why do you come here?' he demanded.

Others, less brave, began to crowd behind him. The Ash Bearer could not move around Luke now, even if she wanted to – which she did not.

'I come in peace,' the lady said. 'Let me go in peace.'

'First tell me who you are,' Luke ordered, his confidence growing now that he no longer stood alone, now that he had heard her voice – soft and low. 'And tell me whose ashes you carry and why you carry them.'

The Ash Bearer regarded Luke steadily, never blinking. Her head moved slightly as she turned to look at the very old and the very young who also barred her way, standing behind Luke. There were babies in their mothers' arms, and vigorous men, and strong young women.

'Let me pass,' the Ash Bearer said quietly.

Luke bent to pick up a rock and the others behind him and behind the Ash Bearer did the same, their eyes feverishly bright. 'Answer my questions and I'll let you pass.'

'I am the Ash Bearer. I do not seek trouble. I seek peace . . . I seek acceptance. Let me pass.'

'Whose ashes do you hold in your urn? A lover? A husband?' a new voice asked. Lower murmurs asked the same question.

The Ash Bearer did not answer. What could she say that would be believed by these people? She had told the truth so many times, only to be spat at and stoned, only to be destroyed and therefore to have to destroy. She was tired, bone tired, blood tired . . . and heartsick. Tired of travelling and tired of new cities, new villages, new faces and always the same old attitudes.

Luke walked towards her, his eyes gleaming greedily. 'What do you live on? You carry nothing but your urn. I don't believe it holds ashes. I smell gold, jewels.'

The Ash Bearer clutched her urn even closer to her.

'Give it to me!'

'I won't. I can't.' The Ash Bearer said sadly, but she knew that she was going to lose here, just as she had lost everywhere else.

Luke turned back to his followers. 'Grab her! Hold her my friends. She carries riches for us all. I know it!'

The Ash Bearer was quickly knocked to the ground, numerous hands holding her down. 'Don't open it. *Please*, don't open it.' The Ash Bearer tried to speak through the blood in her mouth.

Luke had the urn and a hush fell on the crowd. With an avaricious flourish, Luke lifted the lid on the urn, bending his face over it.

The Ash Bearer closed her eyes, forcing the scream in her stomach to rise, willing it to escape, to be heard. Finally it came. A howl to chill the blood . . . had there been anyone to hear her. Then came the weeping . . . so sorrowful . . . The Ash Bearer stood up, wiping her eyes with the back of her hand before looking around. There was nothing and no one in sight. Just her covered urn, her bottomless urn, filled with ashes, filled with souls. Slowly she picked it up – much heavier now, as she knew it would be – and continued her solitary walk.

Murderous Shadows

If you won't come back to me then leave me alone. Stop it! Stop following me . . . What was I supposed to do for heaven's sake? That swine had me declared insane and locked up like a wild animal. He knew I was as sane as anyone . . . as sane as *he* was. With hindsight I can now see that a lot of it was my fault. Everything he did I did better and faster – art, pottery, writing poetry, reading, mathematical theorising – everything. There was only one thing I was stupid about . . . not concealing that I knew more than him. And in a world where men rule and women do the few jobs that the robots cannot do, that was worse than stupid.

But I thought he loved me. He told me my brown skin was soft like the finest gossamer silk. (Mum used to say it was like sandpaper.) He told me my brown eyes shone like stars in a clear sky. (Mum used to say I had eyes like a dead goat.) He told me my brain was a finely honed instrument which he admired. (Mum used to say I was totally dizzy.)

I believed him. (I believed her too. After all women perceive these things differently from men. That doesn't mean that either perception is wrong.)

But after four years of living with him I guess I must have been right in one argument too many. On my birthday, which was also our anniversary, the Custodians came for me and I was committed. I'd rather he'd had me killed. Four whole days passed before the

warden of the 'Hole', as it was known, told me why I
had been imprisoned.

'He ordered it.'

'Why?'

'No reason was given.'

'How long do I have to stay here?'

'Indefinitely.'

'Where exactly am I?'

'The Rehab asylum for Category A deviants.'

Pause.

'I see . . . What happens now?'

'He has ordered that you be confined to solitary for a
few years. You've got on the wrong side of a powerful
man, but maybe . . . in time . . .'

I don't believe in maybe. I've never believed in maybe.

So into solitary I went. I had one wall-light by the
door which was on continuously and, if I broke it, I
wouldn't get another one. Not ever. I was luckier than
most though, I could have books and an audio-visual
unit. I rarely used the books or the AVU . . . I didn't
want the gifts of an uneasy conscience.

I talked to you instead. At first I was hardly aware of
you, you were just there. Always. But slowly, surely, I
began to realise that you were with me and would never
desert me. You kept me warm at night by sleeping with
me and cool by day by leaving me alone. That's when I
began to talk to you. You never replied but you always
listened. Then I realised that I didn't have to say a word.
You could read my mind, you *were* my mind. I was you
and you were me. So I sat still and smiled at you, hour
after hour, day after day.

I concentrated on you, and you began to separate
from me. Little by little, picometre by picometre.

And I sat silent, and smiled. Of course we were
careful to make sure that the Custodians always saw us
together, with you as impassive, as neutral as they

expected. Only we knew different. After many years you were still me, but now completely separate too. We danced and watched the AVU together.

But I hadn't forgotten *him*. Not by any means. I thought long and hard about how I would be revenged. My plan was simple, ingenious. You would leave by cover of darkness, never coming out during the day unless you could hide in a crowd of your own kind. A crowd where one more shadow would never be noticed. I would close my eyes and feel as you felt, see as you saw. I decided that we would pay him a visit on my birthday, our anniversary. My birthday was at the beginning of summer. Strangely enough it was the first clear summer night we had had all year – or so I was told. An omen?

You would be my ears and eyes. You would breathe the air and the sweet, musky scent of the flowers for me. You could transfer the heat of the pavements and the trees. I loved the summer.

So, on the designated night we waited for the Custodians to pass. You slipped under the door like air or water and were free. I could feel our exhilaration, our joy at getting out of the cell at long last. I lay back on my hard bed and gave my mind entirely over to you. It was a very long journey. You grew tired but we couldn't give up. There was not enough time even to wonder at changes, no room for admiration of the new or the old. To do so would be to allow ourselves to be deflected from our purpose. Three long, hard nights and a day it took to reach him. But it was worth it. Every time I think of what we did to him I smile. He deserved it. He hid my light in a prison. *He deserved it.*

I remember the look of terror on his face. He understood immediately . . . he always was fast on the uptake. Not as fast as me, but fast enough. We killed him slowly, a wound for every month I'd been imprisoned. My hands moved as yours, your feet moved as mine. We were superb. We were supreme. And he died . . . as he deserved.

But you didn't come back to me. Why? I wanted you back. I *needed* you back. With him dead and no proof against me – how could I have done it? I was in prison. So I was set free – no complainant, no complaint. But you didn't come back. I can feel you close to me, watching, following. I see through your eyes, you see through mine. I know I disgust you. I have to keep moving now. I cause pain. I maim and kill, but I only do these things because you didn't come back to me. You were the one who kept me under control. I thought you were my shadow.

I realised too late that you were my soul.

Child's Play

It was Sunday. I had been at the new school for exactly one day and I wasn't sure I liked it. I decided that I wanted to be by myself so I went for a walk in the park. I still missed my old school, Towervale, and all my old friends and I didn't see why I had to move to Almane Primary, even if it was a lot closer, but Dad had insisted and so that was that. Elli seemed friendly, I liked her, but some of the others in the class had spent that first day giving me some very strange looks. Thankfully my first day had been a Friday, so at least I had a break before I had to go back again.

'You're the new girl aren't you?'

I looked at the girl who had stepped directly in front of me. I recognised her as a girl from my class, Susaine, I think her name was.

'Anita isn't it?'

'That's right,' I replied.

Beside her was another girl from my class, Tina. Elli had told me that Tina was all right on her own – in small doses – but Susaine was a bully.

'How well can you fight?'

I frowned, 'Pardon?'

'How well can you fight?' Susaine repeated with impatience.

'I don't know,' I replied, watching first Susaine and then Tina, What a strange question. I'd only fought with the twins and on the odd, rare occasion with my older sister Ellen, so they didn't count.

Then I realised what was coming next. 'I want you to fight Tina,' Susaine commanded.

'She hasn't done anything to me,' I said carefully. 'Why should I fight her?'

'Are you a coward?' Susaine mocked.

I straightened my back. 'No I am not. I just don't pick fights for no reason.'

'So you won't fight her?' By this time, there were a few more people around us, listening to every word. Some of them I recognised from the playground at Almane. I couldn't let them think that I was a coward . . . because I wasn't.

'I won't start it,' I said slowly, now realising that win, lose or draw, I had to show the crowd that I wasn't a coward.

'Hit her Tina.'

I stared at the other girl. She was my height and pretty, with corn-rowed hair plaited back off her face. Would she really hit me because Susaine told her to? Surely . . . She pushed me – hard – on my left shoulder. I pushed her back.

'Fight, fight!' someone around us shouted, and within seconds we were surrounded. Tina pushed me again. I pushed her as hard as I could so that she had to step back to keep her balance. Then she punched me and we were at it.

I slapped and pinched and kicked, but I was losing. Again and again she punched my face whilst I was too slow to block many of the punches. Soon I was on the grass, clambering desperately to get to my feet. I grabbed Tina's leg and bit as hard as I could.

I was losing and with only one thought: *Don't cry Anita. For God's sake don't cry*.

It was the Park Keeper who finally separated us. My nose was bleeding and my face throbbing. I blinked rapidly to stop the tears from escaping my eyes and turned to look at Susaine. She had a smile of intense satisfaction on her face.

'Are you all right?' Tina asked me.

I nodded slowly, not wanting to shake the tears loose. *Don't cry Anita*. I didn't have to ask Tina if she was OK. There wasn't a mark on her.

'Come on Anita – I'll get you cleaned up.' Tina took me by the arm and we followed the Park Keeper down the hill to a small wooden hut in the children's playground. He damped a small, pale-blue towel before saying crossly, 'Tip your head back and hold this to your nose.' I tilted my head back although Tina took the towel before I had the chance and held it to my face.

'For Gawd's sake, why the bleedin' hell were you two fighting?' asked the Park Keeper. 'Just look at the two of you now!' Neither of us said a word. After a short while my nose stopped bleeding. Tina rinsed out the towel before hanging it back on its hook.

'Thanks Mister.' Tina smiled. I didn't feel like smiling – far from it.

'I'm sorry Anita,' Tina said sincerely, trying to take my arm again once we were alone.

'Then why did you do it?' I drew away from her. I looked up the hill. There was no one there now, not even Susaine. Everyone was here – following the word 'FIGHT'! – and then gone with the wind. Tina looked uncomfortable, miserable.

'Susaine is my friend. She . . . every new girl has to . . . I've only been hammered once – by Susaine herself – so everyone's afraid of her. She only does it to see where you fit in. Nothing else will happen now.'

I stared at Tina with disbelief. 'So you fight every new girl because Susaine tells you to . . . because she's set up some kind of fighting league table.'

Tina shrugged.

'Why on earth do you do it?' I asked angrily.

'I've got no choice, Susaine . . .'

'Don't be ridiculous! Of course you have a choice.'

'I don't,' Tina said earnestly. 'Susaine knows . . . we were at Infants together. She used to live in my street. She knows . . .'

I looked at her. She wasn't going to say any more. The way she repeatedly kicked at the grass showed me that she thought she had already said too much.

'Come on,' I said. 'Let's get an ice-cream.'

'I don't have any money.'

'I do,' I said. Tina linked her arm with mine and we walked off, and I thought, 'I'll get you Susaine. You just see if I don't.

'You must promise not to say a word to anyone.'

Elli and I turned to each other, eyes wide. 'We promise,' Elli said quietly.

'You must swear by the power of the Secret Forest,' Janet persisted.

'Secret Forest my eye,' I scoffed. 'It's only a few dozen trees in the park.'

'Shut up Anita,' Elli snapped. 'If you're not going to enter into the spirit of the thing . . .'

'I promise,' I interrupted quickly.

It was just past sunset and the sky was a sleepy, deep blue. I looked around. This was *so* creepy! The Secret Forest was full of strange sounds and long shadows, creeping, scuffling around us. I wished Janet would hurry up and tell us Susaine's secret so we could leave. Janet regarded each of us in turn before she spoke again.

'I know this is going to be hard to believe but it's true. Susaine isn't like us. She's not . . . well, she's not from this planet . . .'

'Well *I* could've told you that,' I frowned. 'Come on Janet, get to it!'

'I'm serious. Susaine's from another planet.'

I sat back disappointed. 'Don't talk wet,' I said scathingly. And here I'd been looking foward to a juicy secret.

'I'm serious,' Janet replied angrily. 'And what's more I can prove it.'

'Go on then,' Elli challenged, as disappointed as I was.

'She doesn't have any blood.'

Silence.

'WHAAT?!' I asked, not sure that I had heard correctly.

'She doesn't have any blood,' Janet repeated triumphantly.

'She told you this, did she?' Elli mocked.

'She did actually.' Janet was annoyed now. It was obvious that none of us believed a single word. 'Two years ago, I went to her house for her birthday party and when I arrived, her Mum said that she was in the kitchen. I walked in to say hello . . . She was cutting up sandwiches and I saw the knife slip. It chopped into her finger . . . but no blood came out.'

'What did come out then?' Elli asked.

'Green gunk with purple spots, I'll bet,' I said sarcastically.

'Nothing came out,' Janet interrupted. 'That's just the point. She cut into her skin quite deeply . . . but there was no blood . . . *nothing*! That's when she saw me.'

Silence.

'What happened then?' Tina asked.

I nudged Elli, nodding towards Tina. Tina was so gullible! If she was told that the sky had turned lime-green she would believe it without checking it for herself first.

'You don't believe this rubbish do you?' I laughed.

'Shut up Anita,' Tina snapped. 'What happened then Janet?'

'Well,' Janet said slowly. 'She told me to come closer and to shut the door behind me.'

'And you did what she said.' Elli smiled with disbelief. 'After all, it's not every day that you meet someone with a hollow finger!'

'Do you want to hear this or not?' Janet was *really* annoyed now. We shut up.

'She said she had replaced the real Susaine when she was only five. The real Susaine is on her planet being studied. She – *our* Susaine – will be here on Earth until she's 50, although she'll stop ageing at 23.'

I stifled a snigger. Janet gave me a filthy look before continuing. 'She doesn't have bones or blood and it doesn't matter what happens to her here on Earth because she can't die. There's nothing on Earth that can kill her.'

'Except one of Anita's jokes.' Elli laughed.

The shadows around us grew longer, colder.

'I'm serious. I swear to you on the Bible . . . on my mother's life that I'm not lying.'

'Let me see your fingers and swear again,' I said suspiciously. Janet held out her hands to me, her fingers outstretched so that I could see she didn't have them crossed as she repeated her promise that she wasn't lying.

'What happened then?' Tina asked.

'Tina, you don't honestly believe this shit do you?' Elli asked incredulously.

Elli was so sophisticated, using words like S--T. I don't swear. If Mum caught me swearing she'd whip off her slipper . . . 'Swearing is too common, gal. Don't do it!' she'd say, applying her slipper to my bum with a vengeance!

'*What happened next*?' Tina repeated, ignoring Elli and me.

'I asked her why she was telling me this,' Janet said. 'But all she said was that she could use me. She *needed* people like me to succeed. God I was frightened . . . I couldn't move.'

'Why didn't you tell someone?' I asked.

'Like who? Who would believe me? It's true but there's no way I could convince people that I was telling the truth. I've never told anyone what I saw or what she said . . . until now.'

'Too right,' I scoffed. 'You don't want to be carted off to the funny farm.'

'It's true damn it! She doesn't have any blood or bones. When she's 50 she'll disappear back to where she came from and then you'll believe me.'

'Can we wait that long?' I asked Elli, trying desperately not to burst out laughing.

'I don't think so somehow!' Elli said.

Janet was furious. 'All right then. We'll just have to prove it, but you lot will have to help me. We'll have to trip up Susaine in the playground and cut her and when she doesn't bleed you'll all see that I'm right!'

'Yeah, and when her shin or her arm *does* bleed, then she'll demonstrate just how human *we* are by beating the hell out of us,' I pointed out. 'No thanks!'

'It's true,' Janet pleaded. 'I would try to cut her myself but she knows that I know about her . . . she can probably read my mind. It wouldn't surprise me.'

I had to hand it to her, Janet was very convincing.

'One of you will have to do it. I can get a kitchen knife and I'll help to hold her, but one of you must cut her and then we can tell Mrs Bleasdale and she'll tell the police and they'll take Susaine away. We'll have to cut her somehow, tripping her up is too hit and miss.'

34

'Tina,' I frowned, 'did you know any of this, about Susaine not having any blood?'

'No I didn't,' Tina replied earnestly. 'But it doesn't surprise me. I always knew that there was something funny about Susaine.'

'What are we going to do?' Elli asked, serious now for the first time.

'Well . . .' Tina began uncertainly, 'we . . . could perhaps do something like Janet suggested.'

'*Who'll cut her*?' I asked. 'I can't do it. If she does bleed, she'll hammer me into the ground. You were bad enough Tina!' I reminded her. Tina squirmed a little, looking embarrassed. *So you should squirm, Tina*, I thought.

'*I'm* not going to cut her. I can hardly fight my way out from under my blanket each morning,' Elli said, making us all laugh. 'God knows, it didn't take Tina long to wipe the floor with me when I first joined Almane, Susaine would pulverise me!'

'Which leaves you Tina,' Janet pointed out. We all looked at Tina.

Janet continued. 'Honestly Tina, once you've cut Susaine and no blood appears, she'll have to leave you alone . . . she'll have to leave all of us alone because we'll know about her. When it was just me who knew the truth, Susaine had me under her thumb . . .'

'Safety in numbers,' I muttered.

'Exactly,' smiled Janet.

'All right, let's do it,' Elli said with determination. 'But Tina, you'd better bring your own knife, just in case Janet can't sneak one from her home.'

'OK,' Tina agreed. Even in the fading light I could see Tina's eyes shining at the thought of getting back at Susaine. And the shadows around us grew longer.

'OK, you three hide around by the toilets,' I said. 'I'll get Susaine over there.'

'How?' Elli asked.

'I'll think of something.' I frowned. I hadn't worked that part out yet. 'Just be ready to grab her, and don't look into her eyes. We don't know for sure what sort of powers she has.'

From the time we had arrived at school that morning, we had discussed nothing else. Elli and I were prepared grudgingly to admit that maybe Janet was right. 'Susaine is very strange and she *is* wicked,' we said to Tina. 'And Janet *did* swear on a Bible that she was telling the truth.'

Tina had brought her mum's meat knife to school, hidden in her coat pocket (which was just as well because Janet's mum caught Janet fishing through her cutlery drawer). We were all frightened but determined to expose Susaine for what she was. Then she'd leave us alone.

'Or maybe,' Tina said, 'we could use her to do things for us . . .'

The plan was somehow to lure her into the alcove just behind the girls' loos. No one ever went there because it was too smelly, so it was ideal. I waited until I saw Janet, Tina and Elli walk around the corner in to the alcove before I walked up to Susaine. My mouth was dry and I could actually hear my heart pounding. Susaine was pushing Floyd, a small, slim boy in our class, against the wall. I grabbed her arm.

'Why don't you pick on someone your own size?' I asked her. Floyd scarpered, without saying one word.

'Are you serious?' she asked, obviously amazed at my courage . . . or stupidity.

I let go of her arm. 'Yes I am. I haven't forgotten the way you set Tina on me. You've set Tina on everyone . . . Elli, Karen, Janet, Pamela, Julie . . . like she was some sort of pet Alsatian. Well, I've had enough of it. This time it's your turn.'

'Whenever you're ready.' Susaine's voice was husky with confidence.

'All right then,' I replied slowly. 'You and me, behind the loos.'

'What's the matter with right here?' she asked sarcastically.

I was scared . . . no, I was petrified. 'So you can get one of your creepy crawlers to help you when you start losing?' I mocked. 'Forget it.'

'You must be joking!' Susaine's laugh was a dog's bark. 'I could mop the floor with you with one hand behind my back.'

'Prove it then!'

Without another word Susaine turned and headed for the toilets, her expression set as she walked slightly ahead of me. I let her go a few paces in front before I ran up to her and pushed her as hard as I could. Unfortunately it wasn't hard enough, she kept her balance. I raced for the loos. If Susaine caught me before I reached them, I'd be history! I ran faster than I'd ever run before, knowing that Susaine was only a few steps behind me.

'She's here!' I screamed, darting into the alcove. Janet, Tina and Elli suddenly appeared. Susaine pulled up short but before she could turn around, we all grabbed her.

'You swines!' she shouted. 'Four against one, you're all . . .'

Elli put her hand over Susaine's mouth, her other hand around Susaine's neck whilst Janet and I wrestled to keep Susaine's legs and arms under control. Elli was behind Susaine, Janet and I on either side of her. Tina stood in front of her, knife in hand. In the spring sunshine the blade seemed to be winking at us.

'Come on Tina, hurry up,' Janet hissed. 'We can't hold her for much longer.' Susaine was struggling even more frantically now, screaming words that were smothered by Elli's hand. I had to use both arms and my leg wrapped around Susaine's to try and keep her still. Janet had to do the same. With a quick glance at each of us, Tina stepped forward.

'Stab her, *stab her*,' Elli ordered.

'Stab her, come on,' Janet demanded.

'Hurry up Tina,' I hissed.

Biting her lip, she plunged the knife into the right side of Susaine's chest. There was a strange gurgling sound as Susaine stopped struggling, staring down at the red patch spreading over her yellow T-shirt. We instantly released her. She sank to her knees and then fell in slow motion to the ground, her face on Tina's shoes. Tina stared at her, her mother's knife still in her hand. It glistened, shining wet with blood like freshly applied red paint. We screamed and screamed. Tina didn't move. She just stood there, staring at Susaine. Within seconds there were more girls around us and instantly more screaming. Then more and more kids arrived followed by the teachers, Mrs Bleasdale leading them.

'It was . . . it was Janet.' Tina's voice was low, strange, almost a whisper. Only a few of us heard her.

'It was Janet,' Tina said, the knife still in her hand. 'She said Susaine didn't have any blood . . . she said Susaine was an alien.'

Janet was crying. 'I never said any such thing Miss. She's lying.' Elli and I were crying too.

'She's dead Miss,' I sobbed. I could just tell she was dead.

'Oh my God!' Mrs Bleasdale breathed. Funny, but that's all she kept saying . . . 'Oh my God! Oh my God!'

Of course the police and an ambulance were called and Tina and Susaine were taken away. When the ambulance men moved Susaine, the front of her T-shirt was nearly all sickly red and the gravel beneath her body was shining a dark red-brown now. I suddenly felt sick. Tina was shaking and crying and staring at Janet, at all of us. But she didn't speak. I don't think that she *could* speak. She was trying to understand. Poor thing! I *almost* felt sorry for her.

Everyone in our class was sent home. Elli, Janet and I went to the Secret Forest, none of us saying a word until we got there. We walked about for a few minutes, searching to make sure that there was no one around. Then we sat down on the ground. It felt cool, almost damp. I wondered how many tiny insects were now scuttling around under the seat of my skirt. How many had been squashed?

'Well it worked,' Elli said, a slow smile spreading over her face. Janet laughed. 'No more Susaine, no more Tina. That'll teach Tina to do Susaine's dirty work.'

'I always swore I'd get even with those two one day,' Elli grinned.

'Mind you, I didn't really expect Tina to kill her. I thought she'd cut Susaine's arm or face . . . teach her a lesson, show her that we would all stick together against her. That's why I started crying . . . all that blood. Yuk! Mind you I'm not sorry she's gone.'

'I reckon everyone in our year must have said that they'd get even with Susaine – and Tina – at one time or another. Those two are . . . were . . .' (Janet relished the word) '. . . *were* real swines! They both got what they deserved. Hell, if we told anyone we'd be heroes . . . well, heroines at any rate . . .'

'But we can't tell anyone,' Elli interrupted. 'We each swore that.'

'I know, but I still wish we could,' Janet sighed. 'Did you see Tina's face when I was telling her about Susaine

being a creature from outer space!' Janet rocked back
with laughter. '*She's so stupid*. She'll believe any load of
rubbish.'

'Those who think with their fists, believing any shit,
will die by their fists,' Elli delivered reverently. She
nudged Janet.

'You're very quiet Anita.'

I stood up and looked down at the ground I had just
been sitting on.

'I was just wondering how many insects I've crushed,'
I said thoughtfully. 'I hate killing insects.'

Mother to Daughter

Dear Alison,

Happy New Year darling! How are you? I hope that you are well. I guess I'm OK, considering. How is Steve? Give him my love. Have you been cleared to have children yet? I hope so. Nothing would give me greater pleasure than to hold my grandchild. Obviously I can't speak for Steve but there should be very little wrong with *you*. I carried and protected you all through the Trouble . . . but enough of that.

What are your plans for the New Year? What plans do the Committee have? I hope I don't get you into trouble by asking, but I *am* anxious to learn what they have in store for us. Everyone here says that they can't allow us to live much longer, but surely they wouldn't dispose of us so ruthlessly? Surely they wouldn't be *allowed* to get rid of us like so much unwanted rubbish?

I'm sorry to question you about the Committee every time I write, but as Steve is one of their key members I thought perhaps you might have a better idea of exactly what is going on. Obviously, I don't want to get either of you into trouble so, if you can't reply to my questions, please write back anyway and let me know how you are . . . and what you're both doing. What's it like in the outside now? We can't see much from our camp because of the high walls and the roof. The little we do see tends to be just sky . . . through the holes in the roof which are never repaired!

Not that I'm criticising. I'm sure that the Committee

have far more important things on their minds, and as it only affects people like myself who sleep on the top floor, I suppose there is no real cause for concern. It does get a bit cold though and I worry about the rain falling on me.

Christmas day here came and went without incident. It was *almost* like any other day except that a few of us got together in the exercise hall and sang carols to make the day slightly more festive. We didn't really succeed – not really – but we tried. I know the Committee don't like people celebrating Christmas any more but I think they're wrong . . . after all, the Trouble was caused by indifference and hate and Christmas was – is – really the only time of the year when such feelings are put aside, however superficially. Everyone needs something to believe in, some reason to forget their troubles, however temporarily. Oh dear, there I go! Preaching again! Write soon darling. I love you.

All my love,
Mum

4 February

Dear Alison,

How are you? I hope you and Steve are well, and that you received my January letter. I'm still waiting to hear from you, but I think I know why you haven't replied to my last letter. Steve *is* contaminated isn't he? Somehow I know I'm right . . . why else have you not written to me? You must be so upset, distraught. I don't really know what to say to you, I was looking forward to holding my grandchild so much. But *you* must feel far worse than me . . . I mean, at least I had you.

There are a number of options available to you, of course. You could find a surrogate father, or adopt.

How would Steve feel about that? Still . . . even if you don't manage to have a child, at least you have each other. Sometimes, just sometimes, I wish that your father was still alive, then I feel guilty at my selfishness. Really, all things considered, I believe he is better off dead. I wouldn't like him to be here now, to see where I and others like me have ended up . . . I suppose I'm really just waiting to join him. But there I go, being morbid again!

Dennis, my friend, says that I will get my wish sooner rather than later the way the rain pelts down on me when I'm locked up in my cell. I huddle in a corner where the roof is not too bad but it still runs down my face and all over my body. It's terrifying, so icy-cold. Sometimes it feels as though it's freezing my soul. I try to switch off – to divorce my mind from my body – by remembering the days before the Trouble. Days when I was a young English teacher, just married, loving my job and loving your father. Days when there were four distinct seasons instead of the perpetual autumn we have now, always raining and the air so cold. A grey autumn with no colours and no autumn sounds either, just the atmosphere of dying. I disappear back into the past when I can – which helps, until I *have to* return to the present. There is nothing now but the past and the present. I don't have a future, except maybe in you and, hopefully, my grandchildren.

Alison, please come and see me. I miss you very much. And I'm very lonely. I'm not trying to tell you what to do and I'm certainly not trying to make you feel guilty.

You have nothing to feel guilty about, but *please come and see me.*

All my love,
Mum

21 February

Dear Alison,

How are you? I'm dying. I know it for certain. I have a continual cough, and my hands shake so much that I can hardly hold my pen to write this letter. I'm sorry you couldn't get here for my birthday. I had hoped . . . but no doubt you're too busy.

Darling, please visit me. You don't have to stay long. I'd just like to see you again, before I die.

It's strange, but it seems all my friends are dead or dying too. That's not strange in itself of course – not in this hell hole – but we all seem to have got so much worse around the same time. I guess it's the cumulative effect of the rain and the cold. I find myself wondering about the world outside – what it looks like, how it feels. But I don't envy you . . . I used to Alison, but I don't any more. I wouldn't like to live in a world where scapegoats have to be found for the Trouble, because it won't stop there you know. This world learns nothing from the past, and there's no reason for the past to be remembered. How can anyone believe that by locking us up like battery hens nothing similar will ever happen again? You're following the same path that we took; you'll end up as we did. Perhaps not your generation, but it will happen . . . one day. I pray it will. This life I lead has to be for a reason, even if that reason is only to prove that none of us *ever* learns from our mistakes. I try to understand your attitude . . . not yours personally – but the Committee's attitude . . . and the attitude of the others on the outside whom you let get away with their inhuman treatment of us. But I can't, Alison.

You may say that the Trouble was caused by the Older ones, by politicians and dictators and power-hungry groups or individuals who all had one thing in common . . . their age. All old. You call anyone over thirty-five old. Well, not all 'old' people wanted the

44

war. *We weren't all power-hungry or power-mad.*

You throw us old people into these rat-infested prisons for revenge, then call it justice. Your justice is as illusory as our belief that the Trouble would – *could* never happen. I'm sorry to sound bitter darling, but then again . . . maybe I'm not. I'm coughing up blood now. Why won't you come and see me? Just by yourself, just once. It need only be once . . . There's so little time left.

I remember your face smiling up at me when you were a little girl. I remember it so clearly. But I can't really remember what you looked like as you grew older, the images fade and blur. That makes me cry. Are you like me? Do you look like me? Do you think like me? I love you.

Mum

4 March

Dearest, dearest Alison,

I love you. I won't last another day because I don't want to. Don't have children Alison. I don't like to think of you, imprisoned, perhaps in this very cell, writing letters to your children begging them to visit you. I wouldn't wish this on my very worst enemy. Don't have a child.

If the Trouble had anything at all to do with me, I'll see you in heaven. If it had nothing to do with me, I'll see you in Hell. Just as long as I see you.

My love always,
Mum

A dead woman lies on a bed amongst grimy, crumpled, blood-stained letters, letters which never left her. The walls, even the floor, are covered in writing . . . red writing, the red of her own blood.

Soon the room will be cleaned, ready for someone else who has reached their thirty-fifth birthday.

Not So Stupid!

'You are *so* stupid! It defies belief or description.'

I watched Jon, careful to keep my face as blank as possible. God I hated him.

'Put the damned tray down Maureen and try, try, to pay attention,' Jon said impatiently, adding, 'I'll speak in words of two syllables or less so that even you can understand me.'

How galling for someone with Jon's intellect to be forced to marry a dunce like me. I have . . . no . . . I *had* money . . . Jon didn't. He had the ideas, the dreams, but no money and his ideas on time travel were too far-fetched to win support where it counted . . . in hard, fast cash. So he married me – for my money. My father warned me but I didn't listen. It didn't take long for Jon to reveal his true colours however. I gave him the money he required to start his experiments and after that he practically ignored me, emerging out of his shell of a workroom in our basement only to get more money from me.

That was four years ago. My father died two years ago and the money ran out last year, along with my love for Jon. I admit to being old-fashioned in my ideas, I wanted a proper family life with children. If we'd had children it might have been different but Jon said they were too expensive. It's only now that I understand what he meant. Money spent on children couldn't be spent on his useless experiments.

'Put the tray down Maureen,' Jon commanded.

'But your steak will get cold,' I said feebly.

'So what?' he snapped. 'It always tastes like rubber anyway.' God I hated him.

'This is a Dimension vehicle,' he began proudly. It looked like an ergonomically designed chair enclosed in a glass box to me.

'The time display is so simple that even you could use it,' he continued scathingly. 'You set the date and time you wish to visit here, and the date and time you wish to return to here.'

'Why can't you use the one display to set both?' I asked naively.

Jon glared at me. 'Don't ask stupid questions,' he snapped.

Silence.

'Does it work?' I asked timidly.

'*Of course it does* . . . I'd hardly be showing it to you if it didn't.'

'Have you travelled in it yet?' I asked, strangely interested in spite of myself. I thought I had lost interest in Jon and his experiments a long time ago.

'Not yet. I'm about to, though. That's why I'm telling you all of this. My diary and all my notes are in my desk over there. If I don't come back you should pass the information on to Jeff. He'll know what to do.'

'I didn't know Jeff had been helping you with all of this,' I said in surprise.

'He hasn't. This will be the biggest invention since fire, *and* the wheel.'

I understood immediately. Jon didn't want to share the glory with anyone.

I frowned as a sudden thought occurred to me. 'If you haven't travelled in it, how do you know it works?'

'A fair question, for once,' Jon said with sarcasm. 'Well, two days ago I sent Doxon into the past with it.'

Doxon was our collie dog.

'I set up a video camera in the Dimension vehicle to rotate about three hundred and sixty degrees over the space of six minutes. Then the timer was set to bring Doxon back here. Then I analysed the film.'

'How could you set the timer to bring him back *here*?' I puzzled, then shrivelled under the look Jon directed at me.

'Where do you think I sent him?' he asked with contempt. 'The Eiffel tower, the Battle of Troy, Jupiter? Watch my lips Maureen. He was sent through time . . . not space. I set the time display for yesterday. The vehicle disappeared from today and reappeared in yesterday, but it didn't *move* anywhere.'

'So . . . so, it still appeared to be in your workshop?' I said ponderously.

'Exactly,' Jon said.

'Did you see him in your machine yesterday?' I asked, getting confused.

Jon answered excitedly, 'No I didn't, but then I wasn't down there yesterday. I didn't want anything to interfere with the experiment so I kept away, but set up certain experiments to occur at precise times, carefully synchronised with Doxon's arrival and his stay. By recording the synchronised occurrences taking place, the film showed that Doxon actually had arrived. Do you understand?'

I didn't. Not really. But I didn't say so. It seemed very dangerous to me, to mess about in the past when Jon didn't know what the full consequences of his actions could be. But I also knew that there would be no stopping him now. He always complained that whilst he had the ideas, others seemed to have the knack of turning those same ideas into practical, money-making propositions. I believed that Jon failed because he was too impatient, he cut corners to get what he wanted, then blamed others when his sub-standard or lack-lustre inventions failed to capture the imagination. But of course, there was no way I would ever tell Jon my thoughts.

'So, are you going into the past too?'

'No, *I'm* going into the future. I sent Doxon into the future too, after I had analysed the film, and he returned completely unharmed.'

'*When did you do that?*'

'Yesterday, around this time.' Jon shrugged absent-mindedly. Already he had lost interest in telling me any more. 'Just remember that if something happens to me and I shouldn't return, you're to pass on all my papers to Jeff.'

'I'll remember,' I muttered.

Jon opened the door to the vehicle and bent over to set the times on the digital displays.

'What time are you going to visit?' I asked.

'A year from now I think,' Jon said, his back to me.

'Will there be two of you when you reach the future?' I wondered. Jon favoured me with one of his looks.

'Sorry . . .' I mumbled. 'When will you be back?'

'I don't know.'

'But your steak will get cold,' I protested.

Jon straightened up. 'Go away Maureen. You're getting in my way.' He bent down to continue resetting the controls.

Then it happened. The image, the wild idea suddenly popped into my head. Without pausing to think about what I was doing I picked up the steak knife on the tray and plunged it into his back. He slumped forward without a sound. I watched him, my mind perfectly calm. He was dead, I knew that instinctively without even touching him. Just like that. I smiled, then slowly frowned. My new-found freedom wouldn't last very long if I was put in prison for his murder. But I *wouldn't* go to prison for him, I was determined. I tipped Jon into the vehicle, then got in myself. It was cramped and awkward, but I consoled myself with the thought that it wouldn't be for long.

Pushing Jon's sprawling body away with one hand I reset the time displays with the other. I set the destination dial for tomorrow and set the homeward dial for the present. Nothing happened . . . or had something happened already? No, it couldn't have. I'd have felt something . . . surely? I wasn't sure. There was a button to the right. Just in case, I pressed it . . . after all I had nothing to lose. The sudden force pushed me back – *hard* – into my seat. It hurt my chest but was quickly over. I looked around, I was still in Jon's lab. Nothing seemed different. I opened the door and stepped out, then pulled Jon out behind me. He was still warm.

Was I at tomorrow? I looked around expecting proof to leap at me, but there was nothing. Then I saw the dinner I had brought down for Jon on the table. Tentatively I touched the steak. Ice-cold. I smiled, then laughed. For once it seemed as if one of Jon's inventions was going to work after all.

I looked at the steak knife in his back and wondered if I should wipe my fingerprints from its wooden handle. Would a wooden handle hold fingerprints? Anyway, it didn't matter . . . if I brought him food then my fingerprints *should* be on the cutlery and crockery. It would be suspicious if they weren't. I got back into the contraption and pressed the button again. The same force pushed me into my chair, only this time it was more painful because I expected it. Back in the present I wondered what to do with the Dimension vehicle. I didn't want to smash it up, it would be better if it just disappeared. So I set the dials again, this time setting both the destination and the homeward dials for the same time . . . the fourth of the fourth, four thousand, four hundred, and forty-four. Four has always been my lucky number. No-one would ever even know about Jon's invention now! The next problem was how to press the activating button without getting into the vehicle myself. Finally, I put Doxon in, but didn't strap him up as Jon had done . . . sooner or later his paw would touch the button. Whilst waiting I took all Jon's papers from his desk and stuffed them into the furnace, making sure that I covered my tracks. When I turned around from my task at the furnace the vehicle had gone.

I didn't sleep very well that night, which was surprising. I went to bed thinking of Jon and finally dozed off thinking of his sneering face, and was angry to find that when I woke the next morning he was still on my mind. At ten I dressed as brightly as possible and went to the City Library, careful to place myself at a table with at least six other people. I asked different librarians a lot of questions, going out of my way to be noticed, and remembered, by smiling at different people and entering into conversations I would usually run a mile from. And I enjoyed it. To my surprise, the people I spoke to didn't find me boring as Jon had always said they would. In the evening I went to the theatre, careful to start up a conversation with couples on either side of me, and the theatre usherette. I had two drinks at the bar, making sure that the barmaid would remember me by changing my mind about my drink at least four times. Then I went home, knowing that the warmth of Jon's body would prove he'd only been dead for a few hours, and happy that I had established an excellent alibi.

I didn't even go downstairs. I called out Jon's name, waited five minutes then phoned the police. As I stared out of the front window waiting for the police to arrive I remembered all the years I had wasted with Jon, years

I would never have again. And I began to cry. After all it would look very strange to the police if I didn't cry. When they arrived we all went downstairs together.

I don't know what I had expected but when I saw Jon lying there, the strangest feeling came over me. It was only then I realised that I had really done it . . . *I had actually killed my husband*! Before that moment the last two days had seemed clear but unreal, like a vivid dream. I stared down at my husband and the tears dried in my eyes. I had done it. I had killed him, and I would get away with it . . . I deserved some peace and happiness after everything I'd been through. I stared down at Jon and thought savagely, *I'm not so stupid after all, am I darling*?

Then I fainted.

Sensitivity

'How do you feel, Mrs Jennings . . .?'
   'Do you know Philippa Doyle at all, Mrs Jennings . . .?'
   'Mrs Jennings, why do you think she did it . . .?'
   Click . . . flash . . . click . . . flash.
   'What time did you enter the shop . . .?'
   'Do you often leave your baby . . .?'
   Flash . . . flash . . . click . . .
Mrs Jennings stared in confusion at the auto-press robots swarming over her front path, her front garden . . . constantly moving, shouting at her, shouting at each other. Robots with television cameras, microphones, flash guns instead of blood. Swarming, shouting.

'Hello George, how are you today?'
   'Fine Mrs Jennings, just fine. And yourself?'
   'Not too bad.'
   'Where's Curtis?'
   'Outside in his push-chair. He's been driving me crazy all day, bawling his bloody head off.'
   'What's the matter with him?'
   'He's teething, and keeping me and Matthew up all night, every night.'
   'It'll soon pass.'
   'Not soon enough as far as I'm concerned . . . I'm exhausted. If I don't get a good night's sleep soon, I shall keel over.' Mrs Jennings ran a shaky, self-conscious hand through her lank hair, acutely conscious of how

bedraggled she must look. Blood-shot eyes surrounded by dark circles; head bent forward, shoulders drooping in a very unattractive figure of weariness.

'Oh well, I'd better get on.' She shrugged, 'I'll have a pound of steak and kidney please George.'

'Coming right up.'

The purchase paid for, Mrs Jennings made her way to the door. She was very tired, and the late night quarrels between herself and Matthew were not helping matters either. They had agreed to share the night feeds and nappy changes, but it wasn't working out that way. Matthew complained that he had to go to work so he needed his sleep.

'And what's that supposed to mean? Do you think I spend all day in this house doing sweet FA?' Mrs Jennings remembered saying.

'Don't start on at me Angela,' Matthew snapped. 'I've had a long hard day.'

'My day has been longer and harder . . . at least you've had proper company. The only person I talk to is Curtis. Another year of this and I'll be ga-ga.'

'Don't be ridiculous Angela. Look, I'm going out for a while.'

'Well, thanks a lot. That's right. Just run away. And whilst you're running just be bloody grateful that you can. I can't.'

Mrs Jennings shut the shop door behind her with a sigh. Ever since Curtis was born all she and Matthew had done was argue about trivia. But trivia had a way of gnawing at you just as voraciously as the so-called more important things. Mrs Jennings turned to Curtis, relieved that for once he had stopped crying.

He wasn't there.

Mrs Jennings moved quickly around the push-chair.

He wasn't there. She looked up and down the empty street fighting desperately against the tide of disbelief and panic that was rising within her.

'Curtis . . .' she whispered. 'Curtis, CURTIS,' she screamed.

George appeared from his shop, taking in the scene of an ominously empty push-chair and Mrs Jennings, wild-eyed and hysterical, all in one glance. 'Mrs Jennings! Mrs Jennings . . . calm down. I'll call the police.'

She didn't hear him. Her head, like a jerky puppet's, moved first this way, then that, seeking, staring. Panic turned to acid fear, a fear she could taste like bile in her mouth.

'Mrs Jennings . . . *please*. Come into the shop while I phone for the police.' George placed his hand on Mrs Jennings' shoulder. His hand was slapped away by the now frantic woman. Her mouth opened, issuing no sound at first until she tilted her head back. Then she screamed like a tortured animal. George was horrified. He rushed back into his shop and phoned for the police.

'What's his name Mrs Jennings?' Silence.

'Curtis. His name is Curtis,' George answered finally when it was obvious that Mrs Jennings would not, or could not.

'How old is he . . .'

'Around eight or nine months,' George answered immediately this time. 'He's teething.'

'Mrs Jennings?' The policeman said gently. 'Mrs Jennings? Can you answer some questions?' Silence.

'Look Mr . . . Mr?'

'George, call me George.'

'OK George, do you know Mrs Jennings' address?'

'No I'm afraid I don't.'

The policeman standing by George turned to the policewoman seated beside Mrs Jennings. 'You'd better look in her handbag,' he said after a quick glance at the silent mother. 'See if you can find her address while I go and issue a bulletin from the car.'

He returned five minutes later and obviously not a moment too soon if he read the butcher's expression correctly. George was shifting uneasily from foot to foot, unsure of what to do or say, the frown on his face clearly displaying his discomfort.

'Have you found an address?'

'Yes,' the policewoman answered. 'She's got a credit-card bill here with her address on it, and some keys in her handbag.'

'What about her husband's work address or telephone number?'

'No, that's not here, but it might be at her house.'

'Well, our next step is to take her home I guess. We'll phone her husband, and a doctor, from there,' the policeman stated. 'Mrs Jennings . . . Mrs Jennings, we're going to take you home now. Can you hear me Mrs Jennings?'

'Come on dear.' The policewoman stood, gently pulling Mrs Jennings to her feet, 'We'll get you home and call your husband. Don't worry. You'll soon have your son back safe and sound.'

'That's right Mrs Jennings. We'll soon have him home.' The policeman smiled with confidence as he escorted her out of the shop.

'Mr and Mrs Jennings, I'm . . . I'm sorry but . . .' The inspector stumbled over the words. Mrs Jennings stared straight ahead from her seat on the sofa. Matthew, who had only just arrived home, sat next to her. They didn't touch each other, and they didn't speak. Slowly Mrs Jennings looked up at the inspector's face but couldn't really see it. He was standing in front of the net curtains, with the sunlight flooding in through the window. It made him seem dark and faceless, a shadow with a voice. There was no sound but the ticking of the clock over the mantelpiece and the inspector stumbling over his words. Tick . . . tick . . . tick . . . So still, so calm. Tick . . . tick . . . tick . . .

'We've found Curtis. He's dead I'm afraid. I would like to extend my sincerest condolences.'

'How did he die?'

Mrs Jennings turned to look at her husband. Why was he speaking so strangely? His voice was soft, so far away . . . like a voice whispering down a long, quiet tunnel. She turned back to the inspector. His voice had the same quality. They really should speak normally, her head was hurting from straining to hear them.

'We have the woman who did it.' The inspector went on, 'She's . . . she's made a full confession. She saw the child alone and just picked him up . . . to take him for a walk is what she said. He started crying and she became frightened so she . . . she tried to shut him up.'

'What did she do?' Matthew asked grimly.

He's crying, Mrs Jennings thought with wonder. *Why is he crying?*

The inspector took a deep breath. 'She . . . she hit him . . . battered him. I'm so sorry. One of you . . . Mr Jennings, could you possibly come down to the hospital to identify your son please?'

'I can't leave my wife,' Mr Jennings replied after a pause. 'Not until the doctor comes anyway.'

'Of course, of course. I understand.'

At that moment the door-bell rang. Mrs Jennings remained seated on the sofa whilst her husband left the room to open the front door. She heard faint, inaudible whisperings from the hall – more low, husky voices. Doctor Sinclair entered the room followed by Matthew.

'Hello Angela,' the doctor said gently. Mrs Jennings wondered why he looked so sad. It was a beautiful day,

58

sunlight filling the room, shining on her face and hands and feet. Strange that it was so cold though but maybe not that strange considering that it was autumn. Autumn was always bright days but cold winds.

'Angela, I'm just going to give you a sedative . . .' The doctor opened his bag as he spoke.

'I don't need a sedative Doctor Sinclair,' Mrs Jennings told him with a faint smile. 'I just want to be on my own for a while. I shall go to sleep whilst Matthew goes to the hospital with the inspector.'

The doctor regarded her speculatively. 'I think a sedative would be best Angela and it *would* help you to sleep.'

'I don't need any help sleeping thank you,' Mrs Jennings replied firmly. 'I'm tired. I shall go to bed now.' She stood up to emphasise her words.

'I really do think . . .'

'I don't need one.'

Mrs Jennings marched out of the room and went upstairs to her bedroom. She went straight over to the bay window, standing behind the net curtains as she watched people and cars pass as normal. Nothing had changed.

'Angela darling, you try and sleep . . . I'll be back in a couple of hours.' Mrs Jennings did not jump or turn around at the sound of her husband's voice.

'All right dear,' she responded quietly. Five minutes later she was in the house on her own. She watched as the men left together, the doctor getting into his car after speaking for a few moments to Matthew. Then Matthew got into the police car and they all drove away, and only then did Mrs Jennings lie down on her bed and stare up at the ceiling.

Two hours later the door-bell rang and rang. Mrs Jennings emerged from her reverie slowly, the insistent peal of the door-bell bringing her back to reality.

Matthew must have forgotten his keys. He was always forgetting his keys. She made her way downstairs and wearily opened the front door . . .

'How do you feel Mrs Jennings . . .?'

'Did you know Philippa Doyle at all Mrs Jennings . . .?'

Click . . . click . . . flash . . .

Mrs Jennings stared at the auto-press robots before her.

'Your baby . . .'

Click.

'Left outside . . . shop . . .'

Click.

'Philippa Doyle. . .'

Flash.

'Your baby . . . battered . . . left outside the butcher's shop . . . how long did you leave him? . . . Philippa Doyle . . . your baby . . . your baby . . .'

Microphones were multiplying under her nose. She stepped back from them, but they quivered nearer. She stepped back again, they followed her. Black ones, silver ones, grey ones . . . following her, condemning her. And the noise . . . and the tinny, shrill, insistent voices . . .

'What are your feelings . . .?'

'Aware . . . held Curtis up by his legs and swung him against a brick wall . . . are you aware. . .?'

'I only . . . left him for . . . for a second,' she whispered. The microphones came nearer, straining to catch every word.

'How are you feeling . . .? your baby . . . how do you feel at this moment. . .?' Mrs Jennings started to smile, then to laugh, then to roar with laughter.

Click . . . flash . . . click . . . flash. . .

'Angela, ANGELA! Let me get past. Damn it, get out of the way . . .' Matthew fought his way through the robot reporters – no easy job. Mrs Jennings could hear someone laughing. Why was someone laughing? Her child was dead . . . her child murdered . . . The microphones . . . the microphones were laughing . . . and the voices. . .

'Damn them,' Matthew swore, trying to shove the front door shut. 'Damn them all to hell. The press shouldn't be robots, they should be people. At least then they'd show some sensitivity. . .' As Mrs Jennings watched, the sound from Matthew's mouth grew fainter and fainter until she could hear nothing at all. But his lips moved faster and faster and faster and faster. . .

That night Mrs Jennings had a nervous breakdown.

Laughing White-Heart

Then I saw him, watching me as he sat on the huge Chesterfield, holding Elise in his arms like a bouquet of flowers. I knew it was him although he was covered from hair to toe with what looked like a purple-blue, shiny, all-in-one body suit. He looked like a grotesque snake, catching the light, first this way, then that and reflecting it around the room in a series of misshapen shadows. He turned to face Elise, still holding her tightly to him and he was laughing. A laugh as grotesque, as monstrous as he was.

I was mesmerised. It was his eyes . . . he had three: two oval slits set off at an acute angle to each other on the right side of his face and one horizontal oval slit on the left side. And from all three shone a sickly, fiercely-bright yellow light . . . like a bright candle in a dank cellar.

'Help me . . . help me please,' Elise pleaded, the white feather clutched in her hand like a lifeline. I watched Elise. I watched him. I had to do something . . . anything. He was evil – tainting everything he looked at, destroying everything he touched. *I had to do something.*

I ran to Elise and snatched the snow feather from her hand. It writhed and wriggled next to the feather I already held in my hand, before bending slightly and remaining still. He stood, disregarding Elise as she fell to the floor at his feet and instantly I knew I had made a mistake. He had resumed the form of a man, wearing ordinary navy-blue trousers and a white shirt. His face was once again the face of the man I knew, cold and cruel now, and utterly triumphant. I had done exactly what he wanted me to do.

I screamed in terror and turned to run – if he caught me I didn't stand a chance. I raced away, knowing he was only steps behind me and hurled myself up the stairs two and three at a time, stumbling slightly. I heard his monstrous laugh behind me, felt his hot breath scorching my nape. In desperation I dropped one of the two feathers; I had to do something to slow him down. I sensed him scoop it up, hardly pausing before he was after me again. I ran into the first room I came to. A bedroom, *a dead end*! I panicked, looking around in horror . . . he had me now. I faced him, dragging air into my lungs at the very sight of him.

'Give me the feather,' he ordered.

I stretched out my hand towards him slowly. 'Will . . . will you leave me alone if I give you . . .?'

'No don't, DON'T!' Elise screamed. 'It's your only chance. Don't give it to him. . .'

He turned to face Elise who, at the sight of him, turned deathly pale before collapsing and I *knew* she was dead. Something used until no longer of use, then carelessly disposed of. He turned back to face me. My hand dropped to my side, clasping the feather. I didn't understand. It didn't matter what I did to the feather, whether I kept it or tried to get rid of it . . . *nothing* seemed to hurt him, or to get rid of him.

'Come here,' he ordered. I was compelled to do as he commanded, because of the feather's power over me, but I didn't understand. He opened his arms, seemingly to hug me. In a daze, I moved slowly into his embrace, fighting against every step, but my feet moved closer and closer to him until I stood before him, my body just touching his. He closed his arms around me, looking down at me, smiling. His head moved slowly towards mine, his sweet-smelling breath blazing over my face, my lips . . . choking me, like incense. He kissed me, his lips soft and gentle and a cold numbness fanned slowly through my body. The feather's power, I realised desperately. I was now as burning cold as he was burning hot. But the feather's power wasn't enough.

I didn't return his kiss yet I couldn't push him away either. Around me I was aware of the room slowly fading from sight. He was still kissing me when we disappeared altogether. My mind screamed for someone – *anyone* – to tell me what was going on. I didn't understand.

'No!' I screamed, sitting bolt upright in bed, drenched, perspiration pouring down my back. My gasps echoed around the room; I fumbled for the bedside-lamp switch above my head. Immediately I put my hands over my eyes, then over my ears. The same dream again – night after night. Different backgrounds, different settings but always the same outcome. I spent my life running away from *him*, but he always found me . . . he always caught me and took me back. But back to where? I didn't know.

I remembered some of the settings, from times long ago and far away and he always found me no matter what I did. I was going crazy. It had got to the stage now where I was too frightened to even go to sleep. Nothing seemed to help . . . I had tried sleeping tablets, relaxation exercises, even getting blind drunk, but always, *always* he would return. I glanced at my alarm clock on the bedside table. Two-thirty in the morning. I could sleep now, knowing he wouldn't return, but I was still shaking. I got up to make some Horlicks, looking forward even more to my holiday. Elise and I were going on holiday to France and I had decided that if the holiday didn't rid me of these terrifying nightmares, I would see a doctor when I came back. I hated doctors. But it was that, or go quietly insane.

'It looks perfect,' I said with relief as Elise and I looked at our hotel. Hotel de la Fente, even the name sounded romantic. 'I just know this is going to be great. The weather is lovely, the scenery is superb and even my driving hasn't been too bad.'

'That's a matter of opinion,' Elise snapped.

'Oh come on Elise, we're on holiday. Don't be such a grouch,' I said firmly. I wasn't going to let Elise or anyone else spoil my holiday. I'd actually stopped dreaming and a night's uninterrupted sleep had given me a taste of what I had missed for so long. We took our cases from the boot of the car and walked up the stone steps to the open double doors. Elise pulled me into the foyer of the hotel which was instantly dark and cool-smelling away from the sunlight outside.

'Hello ladies. Jennifer and Elise Lauden?' The man who spoke was standing behind the reception desk smiling at us.

'Yes. I'm Jenny and this is Elise . . . how did you know?' I asked, surprised.

'You are the only two guests I am expecting this week. I am Philippe Lumi Gaston. I own this hotel. Do either of you speak French?'

I turned to Elise with a smile. My grasp of French was bad but hers was worse, although we always argued the point. One look at Elise's face told me that she hadn't heard the question; she was drooling. Here we go again!, I thought with a sigh. Mind you, this one wasn't too bad . . . tall, over six feet, quite muscular and hair so black as to be purple. His features were curiously regular for a man, like a flattering painting.

'No, I'm afraid we don't speak French.' I smiled.

'No matter. My English is very good,' Philippe replied. 'If you would like to register, I will then show you up to your rooms.'

'Rooms?'

'We can't afford rooms plural,' Elise explained apologetically. 'We've booked one room . . . with twin beds and a shower.'

'Hotel de la Fente is empty, therefore you may have two of our best rooms for the price of one of our cheapest. Eh *voilà*, it is done!'

'Oh but we couldn't . . .' I started.

'Thank you very much,' Elise smiled, casting a look of impatience at me, 'that's very kind of you. Come on Jenny, let's sign in. Jenny and I are glad to finally be here Philippe . . . may we call you Philippe?' Elise gushed.

'Certainly.' Philippe returned her smile, his gaze moving from me to her and back again. 'I shall do everything I can to make your stay as pleasant as possible. Are you here visiting friends or . . .?'

'Oh no,' Elise smiled, 'we're alone. This is the first time either of us has been outside Paris, but certainly not the last. You'll have to bring Len with you next time Jenny, now that you've seen how lovely it is here.'

I had to smile. I knew when I was being warned off, and Elise wasn't subtle. She knew as well as I did that Len was just a friend. Nothing less and certainly nothing more. Philippe came out from behind the reception desk and picked up Elise's suitcase, holding out his hand for mine.

'It's all right,' I said quickly. 'I can manage.'

Philippe shrugged before leading the way up the stairs. I walked behind him and Elise as they climbed the stairs ahead. There was something strange going on here . . . why was a hotel like this one empty at the height of the tourist season? It certainly looked comfortable and stylish enough, with ornate high ceilings, the paintings throughout the foyer and on the walls, and the elaborately carved balustrades.

'Mr Gaston, did you say that we're the only guests staying here?' I asked doubtfully.

'Unfortunately for me, yes. But this should make your stay even more pleasant.' Suddenly Philippe turned around, smiling, although I noticed that not once – *not once* – did he blink. 'Do you not think so?' He said.

'This is a lot better,' Elise agreed with relish.

'You must both call me Philippe and I hope *you* will allow me to call you Jennifer.' He smiled at me again. 'Such a pretty name.' Without waiting for a reply, Philippe continued upstairs.

'Tell me ladies, what do you intend doing here?'

'Well, we thought we would go for walks, go on picnics, you know, just generally relax, in inexpensive style,' Elise chatted.

'Mr Gaston, isn't it a bit unusual to have a hotel such as this empty at this time of year? Surely you should be bursting at the seams . . . you don't have cockroaches or mice do you?'

'Jenny!'

Philippe laughed. 'No Jennifer, we have no uninvited guests. And yes it is unusual – but not unheard of, surely? Here we are. Elise this is your room and Jennifer, yours is next door.'

I made up my mind then. I definitely didn't like him.

Dinner was a very uncomfortable meal, at least it was for me with Philippe buzzing around us like an angry wasp. Elise of course was lapping up the attention. After dinner Philippe announced, 'I have a surprise present for both of you.'

'Great!' Elise jumped out of her seat. 'I love surprises.'

'I don't,' I reminded her.

'You'll like this one,' Philippe said confidently. 'Follow me.' He led the way out of the dining-room, across the foyer and down some steps to a locked door. We watched as he slipped a neck chain with a single key on it from around his neck and opened the door. 'After you,' he said, stepping to one side. Elise went into the dark room immediately.

'No, after you,' I said with a false smile. 'After all you know where the light switch is.' There was no way I was going to enter that room ahead of Philippe. For all I knew he might lock us in there. Philippe laughed softly, as though he guessed my thoughts, and entered the room, switching on the light. I swayed a little and had to grab hold of the door frame to steady myself. It was the room I saw in my nightmares. The same Chesterfield, the same stone block walls, everything was *exactly* the same.

'Jenny, are you all right?' Elise asked.

'Yes, yes I'm fine,' I said staring faintly at Philippe. Was he the same man who persecuted me so mercilessly in my nightmares? I struggled to remember what the man I had seen so often in my sleep looked like, but the harder I tried the further his image slipped away from me. All I could remember was a 'thing' with three eyes and no face, laughing at me. I looked at Philippe again . . . he was watching me intently, his eyes burning. I looked away.

Pull yourself together Jennifer, I thought angrily. The resemblance this room bore to my dream was coincidence or I had made a mistake. Maybe I'd seen a picture of this place before . . . But I didn't understand. *And* I was scared.

'There is a bird which lives deep in the Amazon jungle . . .' Philippe lowered his voice to speak very softly and slowly, reminding me of the trailer for a bad

B-movie, '. . . known locally as the Laughing White-Heart. He is believed to appear only once every thousand years and even then only for one year. He rises out of the flames to search for his mate and returns with his chosen one at the end of his term on earth.' I was interested in spite of myself.

'His feathers are of the deepest blue except for the feathers over his heart which are whiter than coconut flesh. The local people deem him the most evil creature in their world.' Philippe never took his eyes off me as he spoke.

'The thing that distinguishes the White-Heart from all other birds . . . is that he has three eyes, two on one side of his face and one on the other.' I stared at him, terrified, and I instinctively realised that Philippe knew exactly how I felt.

'I have two feathers from this bird which are . . . sacred.' Philippe picked up a box like a jewellery case from a long shelf against one wall, talking all the while. 'Elise, I want you to have one . . . and your sister too of course.' He opened the box slowly. I stared into it. I already had a white feather like those on display. Its shape, its glare were unmistakable. A feather it seems I'd had forever, kept in a locket around my neck. My father used to say that I came out of my mother's womb holding it. No one knows where it came from but I had it in my hand then and I'd had it ever since. Now here was an exact duplicate in this box.

'Thank you but I don't want it,' I said instantly.

'I insist. Consider it a present. A thank you from me.'

'A thank you for what?' I asked suspiciously.

'A thank you for staying at my hotel.'

'Nonsense. I don't . . .'

'Jenny! Excuse us a moment Philippe.' Elise dragged me to one side. From the look on her face I knew what was coming. 'Jenny for goodness sake. If the man wants

69

to give us a feather then humour him. We might get something knocked off the bill or something worth a bit more if we're nice to him.'

'Don't be so bloody mercenary,' I snapped.

'Don't be such a bloody goody-goody,' Elise snapped back. 'I'm here to enjoy myself, and I'm damned if I'm going to let you ruin it for me. Now if the man wants to give us this stupid pigeon feather, then let him. It won't kill you.' And with that she turned and strode back to Philippe. I had no choice but to follow.

'Thank you Philippe. It's very kind of you,' Elise said as she accepted the white feather. I felt sick with fear. I could feel my heart pounding within me.

'And one for you.' Philippe smiled. He took my hand and put the feather into it. I stared down at it. Nothing. Just a soft tickle on my palm. Maybe I was dreaming after all.

'Thank you,' I muttered, keeping my head bent.

'You're welcome,' Philippe replied.

I didn't need to look at him to hear the smile in his voice. Once I was back in my room, I put his feather straight in the bin, then went for a walk in the grounds seething with anger and resentment. Philippe gave me the creeps and I wanted nothing from him . . . nothing.

A few hours later I was writing a postcard to send to my workplace but I spilt ink all over it and had to throw it away. It was then I noticed that the feather I had thrown in the bin was gone. Immediately I checked my locket for my own feather. The whitest feather I had ever seen until Philippe had shown us his. So white, it hurt my eyes . . . so white, it hurt my heart.

'He's gorgeous! I think I'll seduce him.'

'Elise!'

'Don't be such a boring fart.' Elise sighed, bouncing off my bed to put on her shoes. I'd wanted to discuss our itinerary for the next day but all Elise had on her mind was Philippe, Philippe.

'Jenny, you might have come here to catch up on your sleep but I certainly didn't. And Philippe looks like he has a wonderful body. Did you have a look at his feet? They're an interesting size.'

'Elise, there is absolutely no correlation between the size of a man's feet and the size of his genitals,' I said.

'How would you know?' Elise scoffed. '*You'd* run fifty miles at the sight of a prick.'

'Don't be coarse . . .'

'Don't be such a priggish prude . . .' Elise snapped angrily, and stormed out of my room.

I sighed deeply. Sometimes Elise really got on my nerves. She was totally irresponsible, but in some strange way I envied her the freedom of that irresponsibility. With another sigh I switched off the bedside lamp and snuggled under the duvet. As I drifted off to sleep, I wondered what Elise was doing. If I knew my sister, she was sitting on Philippe's lap by now. He didn't stand a chance!

'Who's there?' I was suddenly awake and aware that I wasn't alone. The room was pitch black, the silence deafening.

'Who's there?' I repeated. The words echoed and died around me. 'Elise is that you? Stop playing silly buggers.' I sat up, reaching out to switch on the lamp, but a hand caught mine at the wrist. With a shriek I tried to pull away.

'Don't be frightened Jenny. I won't hurt you.'

'Philippe? Philippe, what the hell do you think you're doing? *Get out of my bedroom.*'

'Philippe? Who is Philippe? He doesn't exist.' I felt the bed sag as the man who gripped my wrist sat down. I tried to remain calm, tried to plan exactly what I should

71

do. I could scream – that's it, scream. *Who would hear me?* Was Elise next door or somewhere else with Philippe? I knew that the man with me wasn't Philippe – the voice was different, deeper, huskier. This man could be anyone, a drunk, a maniac. His words certainly made no sense.

'If you don't let go of me, I'll scream the roof off,' I said after a deep breath, suddenly pulling my hands backwards as I spoke. I was about to dart off the bed when it happened. *Three pale yellow lights appeared* – almond eye-shaped . . . and I knew that the *thing* had opened its eyes. I could see nothing else. I stared, too horrified to move, too terrified even to breathe.

'I've come for you Jennifer,' he said. 'I've found you again . . . at last. You will never escape me.'

'No,' I whispered. 'Please . . . please . . . not again. *Please* . . .' He pulled me towards him, crushing me against his chest until I could hardly breathe. The familiar sickly sweet smell of his breath fanned my face, my hair. Summoning all my courage, all my strength, I pushed myself away from him. Then I screamed and screamed until my throat was sore and my head hurt.

'Jenny, Jenny what's the matter?' The main light was suddenly switched on. I blinked stupidly at my sister. I looked around for *him* but there was nothing in my room.

'Elise?' I whispered.

'It's all right Jenny. You've had a bad dream, that's all,' Elise said from the door. 'Are you all right? Do you want me to sit with you for a while?'

'No, no,' I stammered, still trying to fathom out what had happened. 'I'll . . . I'll be all right. I just had a bad dream. I think I'll read for a while.'

'Are you sure?'

'Positive.'

'Good, because I have a certain gentleman currently

warming my bed.' Elise grinned. 'I'll see you in the morning.'

I smiled. I couldn't help it. 'Good night Elise. Say good night to Philippe for me. Leave the light on.'

Once the door was shut my smile disappeared. What I had thought was real had been only a dream? But it seemed so vivid. I was confused and still too over-wrought to sleep. Tonight of all nights my dream had taken a different twist, a more frightening twist. At least with my old recurring nightmare I knew for certain that it was only that, a nightmare. But now the realism of what had happened disturbed me. *Maybe I was going crazy.* Maybe I was beginning to smudge the line between fantasy and reality. When we got back to London, I would definitely see a doctor.

The next day, Elise barely said two sentences to me. In fact she went out of her way to avoid me. I knew that it couldn't be embarrassment or shyness, my sister doesn't know the meaning of those words! She barely touched her breakfast and was missing from lunch. Philippe seemed to be rather reticent also. He served us our food and although he was pleasant and talked a lot, nothing much was said. At dinner, I caught Elise staring at me time and time again. Finally, when she was beginning to irritate me, I said, 'Have I sprouted two heads or something?'

'I don't know what you're talking about,' Elise mumbled, looking down at her dinner. I decided to ignore her. Sometimes she got into the strangest moods and the best thing was just to leave her alone. Philippe disappeared to get us our desserts.

'Jenny, keep your white feather with you tonight,' Elise said suddenly. I frowned. She looked afraid.

'Why? What's the matter?'

'Don't say anything to Philippe. Please just. . .' But then Philippe returned.

'What were you saying Elise? Have I missed something?' Philippe asked with a brittle smile.

'I was just saying to Jenny that I hope she doesn't have any more nightmares tonight,' Elise explained quickly. 'Wasn't I Jenny?'

'You had a bad dream last night?' Philippe asked quickly, before I could answer.

'It was nothing to write home about,' I shrugged. I wondered what was going on between Philippe and Elise. Elise was well able to look after herself but she looked . . . well, terrified of Philippe.

'And what was this dream?' Philippe asked me.

'I can't remember,' I lied, annoyed at his asking.

Dinner was not a great success. I went to bed after, deciding that Elise would probably want to be alone with Philippe to make up with him. Philippe had intimated as much when, after dinner, he put his arm around Elise and smiled at me. 'We had a silly quarrel last night over something that . . . that is outside the control of either of us.' He smiled. 'Didn't we Elise?'

'Yes we did,' Elise said immediately.

Deciding against playing the part of gooseberry I said good night and went to bed. I had been reading in bed for less than an hour when I suddenly heard what I thought was a muffled cry and I recognised Elise's voice. Pulling on my dressing-gown I left my bedroom and went next door to hers. She wasn't there. I was about to go back to my room, deciding that Philippe and Elise were obviously somewhere making up and that I was imagining things again, when I heard Elise cry out once more. This time the noise came from downstairs, and it didn't sound like a cry of passion either. I crept down, looking in a few rooms but finding no one, then saw the steps which led down to the cellar where

Philippe had given us the feathers. Slowly I walked towards the steps, hopeless despair creeping over me. Here was my dream, hideously brought to life. I knew what was about to happen but I could no more turn back than I could have flapped my arms and flown to the moon. I walked down the steps and opened the door which I knew would not be locked.

It's taken a long time – hundreds of years in fact – but I understand now. The nightmares, the dreams of *him* are my reality and what I thought was reality is nothing but a dream of a time long ago and far away. He is Philippe and Raging Bear and Chakata and all the other men I have ever known throughout all my lives. In each and every one of my reincarnations he projects a new image to entangle and trap me, to bind me once again to him, to use then destroy anyone near me who may serve his purpose until I am his again.

I hate him. I hate him for what he did to Elise. I hate him for what he did, and still does, to me. I ask him 'Why me?' but he just laughs and never answers. I lie still, waiting. Waiting for my term with him to be over. Waiting for the one thousand years to pass. Then I may leave to begin yet another new life. Then – for a while at least – until I grow to womanhood I shall have some peace. I shall forget. I'll be *free* until the year he comes to look for me . . . again.

Not a day goes past without him asking me to give him back his feather, but how can I? I have nothing else. He says he can't let me go unless I give back his heart, but how can I? All *my* memories lie within this heart too . . . if I return it, I'll have nothing left. *My* memory will be his, *my* existence will become his. I would never escape him, not ever. I would *always* be a part of him. I can't do that, even though holding his heart – the feather – means that I must remember each time I didn't escape . . . Even if the pain of remembering is so great that it tears me apart.

So I lie still, whilst he loves me, feeling the tickle of the feather around my neck – and wait to be reborn.

Detail

The Devil seethed with fury, to be summoned in this way was galling but he had no choice. The Book of Old had been found and the invocation spell had been executed correctly.

'Your wish?' he roared.

Mrs Engell, who stood before him, did not flinch. The sight and sound and smell of the Devil was nothing compared to what she had been through in the last twenty-three years of marriage!

'This coming Friday is my wedding anniversary,' Mrs Engell began. 'At three o'clock precisely I'm going to kill my husband. I'm going to kill him slowly, and painfully.' The woman added with relish, 'And I want you to establish my alibi. I want fifty people to say they saw me, so I *couldn't* have killed my husband.'

The Devil's smile was slow. 'I already have a *modus* which works particularly well in this sort of case. I call it *Duplicates*. As you are, so I shall become.'

'What does *that* mean?' Mrs Engell frowned.

'I shall be your *exact* duplicate, in everything, from two o'clock on Friday until after the deed is done. Fifty people will see me and think it's you.'

'That will do nicely.' Mrs Engell smiled with satisfaction. 'Now go.'

The Devil's many eyes narrowed. He would bide his time. Friday was only two days away.

At three fifty-two on Friday the door bell rang. Mrs Engell flung open the door. It was the police.

'Gosh that was fast. I've only just called you,' Mrs Engell said, wiping her just-washed hands on a towel as she spoke.

'Mrs Engell, you're under arrest.' At least two policemen and four policewomen swooped behind Mrs Engell, pinning her arms behind her.

'What's the charge? I reported my husband dead . . . that doesn't mean *I* did it!' Mrs Engell felt smug, and had trouble hiding it. 'In fact I have fifty witnesses to prove I didn't do it.'

'We're not here about your husband's death,' said the chief inspector grimly, 'you're under arrest for the murder of the police commissioner and we have fifty senior officers who were there at the time to prove that you did it.'

'WHAT!! . . . what did you say?' Mrs Engell floundered.

'Take her away,' the chief inspector said with contempt. Walking down the garden path, she glanced around her, bewildered. It wasn't supposed to happen like this. Then she saw him – an ordinary man, wearing ordinary clothes, watching the scene with ordinary human nosiness. But Mrs Engell knew him straight away.

'You tricked me,' Mrs Engell shouted furiously. She didn't quite know *how* yet but she was sure she was right.

'Duplicates are very simple. And I did explain,' the man replied. He didn't open his mouth but Mrs Engell could hear every word. 'As you are, so I became. As you did, so had I to do . . . after all, I was your *exact* duplicate. I did explain but then that's the trouble with you humans. You never pay any attention to detail.'

Betcham Woods

I guess it started when I deliberately left the path and made my own way through Betcham Woods. I went to Scotland for a long, lonely holiday when the woman I had lived with for nine years walked out on me for another man. I sold the house in London – practically gave it away – and gave Beth half of the proceeds via her solicitor. Then I decided to disappear for a while. I drove to Scotland, staying in B&Bs for a week before getting into the car and driving anywhere, as long as it was away from myself. Beth was . . . is . . . me, myself, I.

I stopped off in the one-road town of Callendar. I found a suitable (i.e. cheap) place to stay and avoided the other residents like the plague. Then I found Betcham Woods. They were high up a hill, just north of the road which made up the town. On my first day at this particular B&B, I opened my window and heard them, whispering to me. After that I spent every day, rain or shine, in Betcham Woods (known locally as the Betchams). The walk was difficult so it wasn't very popular, besides which the weather was dire. It was a cold, unpleasant October . . . suiting my mood. I'd spend each morning buying the food I needed for the day: biscuits, cakes, sandwiches, fizzy water, flat wine. Then I'd march to the woods, my expression set to discourage conversation until I was sure that I was completely alone.

Once in the woods I could relax, secure in the

knowledge that there would be no one to intrude upon my grief and self-pity. But on this particular day when I was feeling lower than ever before, I decided to leave the path deliberately to make *sure* no one could disturb me. Even before I stepped off the path I knew it was a stupid thing to do. The Betchams covered close to one hundred acres, with falls and sharp, steep depressions plunging unexpectedly. But deep inside I welcomed the prospect of getting lost – to be as alone in body as I felt alone mentally. Nine years in a relationship is a very long time.

I walked aimlessly for uncounted hours, smelling the freshness of the wet leaves beneath my feet as well as above me. The overnight rain made the air smell almost new: pure, untainted. The little I could see of the sky beyond the masses of entwined branches was an enveloping grey-white, a perfect backdrop for the rich browns and golden yellows around me. As I walked I became slowly aware of the soft crunching of the leaves under my boots – aware of it because it was the only sound I could hear. I stopped walking, deliberately listening for some noise, any noise, but the silence was overwhelming, an impenetrable hat around my head. I smiled and it felt strange, unfamiliar. My smile faded as I looked around. For the first time in a long time I acknowledged a world external to myself. Taking off my small back-pack, I took out the thermal ground sheet and lay it down over the exposed but fairly level roots of a huge, gnarled tree. I sat, my anorak protecting me from the wet trunk and leaned my head back, closing my eyes. I fell asleep.

The crack of breaking twigs somewhere near woke me. Instinctively I knew that I had slept for a long time; I could also sense that I was not alone.

'Who's there?' I shouted, more annoyed than anxious. I'm over six feet tall and solidly built, I know how to look after myself. I heard another twig crack behind me. 'Who's there?' I sprang to my feet, looking around. Then I saw it. My blood ran cold as I stared. There beyond the trees, a face, half hidden behind high grass and bushes. My mouth opened in horror; I could see enough of it to take a hasty step backwards.

It was the eyes, huge, blood-red surrounding glowing, intense-green irises. Those eyes . . . staring at me, watching me. And around them, scales; huge, mud-green and purple scales. I watched frozen, too terror-stricken to do anything but stare as the thing slowly stood up. It took a step towards me . . . I made a noise – a gasp or a shout . . . then turned and ran. I could hear it running after me, its footsteps soft, padded and I ran faster, gulping air into my lungs. I heard it growl; I heard it roar behind me.

My God, what was it? Something I'd never seen before, not even in my foulest nightmares. I turned my head and saw that it was only a few feet behind, its arms outstretched, its hands grabbing at me. I could smell its breath, hot and foetid on my neck. It clawed, its talons ripping my anorak, my jumper, my shirt . . . scratching me, drawing blood. I lurched forward – and yelled, shouted, screamed, but I don't know whether it was because of this thing pursuing me or because the ground had suddenly and unexpectedly disappeared and I was falling . . .

When I awoke it was slowly, and very painfully. If it hadn't been for the pain in my leg I would have wondered if I'd had a bad dream . . . the worst dream of my life. There was a candle glowing dimly beside me. I looked around without lifting my head, which felt leaden and fuzzy. I was in some kind of cavern or cave, with a high ceiling and dark walls.

'You fell into Betcham's Bowl.'

I struggled to sit up, ignoring the pounding in my head and the painful throb of my leg.

'Who said that? Where are you?' My eyes caught sight of a moving shadow, dim and distant, hugging the walls of the cave. I felt sick with fear.

'Who are you?' I repeated. Then the shadow moved towards me. Panic choked me. Then, to my intense surprise and relief it was a woman, a black woman. She was tall and very beautiful in a unique, strange way. Her expression was sombre, almost grave, but what made me stare were her eyes. They were a vivid moss green, the greenest I had ever seen. We watched each other for several moments.

'How are you feeling?' she asked, smiling suddenly.

'A bit battered,' I replied, confused. 'Where am I? What happened?'

'You're in my home. You fell into Betcham's Bowl. That's where I found you.' Her voice was deep, husky. It flowed over me like honey; slow and sweet. Then I remembered.

'I was running. I was being chased.' God, how could I have forgotten!

'Who was chasing you?' she asked evenly.

'It was . . . it was something . . . a thing from hell. It tried to kill me!' I struggled to sit up. She looked sceptical.

'It's true I tell you. I was chased by a . . . a beast.'

'And what did this beast look like?' she asked with a smile.

Ignoring her humouring tone, I said firmly, 'It was covered in scales – purple and slimy green scales I think – and it looked like . . .' I frowned. '. . . it looked like a cross between a dragon and a gorgon. It was hideous!'

At that she laughed outright. 'My goodness,' she said, stifling her laugh when she saw the look on my face. 'Look Mr . . . Mr?'

'Richard. My name is Richard.'

'Look Richard, I think you weren't looking where

you were going and fell down Betcham's Bowl. *Then*
you dreamt you were being chased by some kind of
monster. Doesn't that sound more reasonable?'

It sounded more reasonable all right but it wasn't
what happened. I was certain of that. The woman
moved closer to me, still smiling.

'I can prove there was some . . . some creature
chasing me,' I said eagerly. 'My anorak . . . I felt the
beast claw through my anorak. I could feel its claws on
my back.'

'Your anorak is torn but you did that when you fell
down Betcham's Bowl, not from any imaginary
monster.' I glared at her.

'You haven't told me your name yet,' I snapped, still
annoyed because she didn't believe me.

'Phreena.'

I looked around the cave again. 'Why did you bring
me here?'

'This is my home,' Phreena shrugged.

'You live here? In this cave?!'

'That's right.'

'By yourself?' There was a slight pause.

'That's right.' She shrugged again.

'Why do you live here?' I asked, lying back down.

'Why not?' She shrugged again. 'I've lived here for a
few years now and I like it. It suits me. It's my home.'

'Surely you could get the Council or some society for
the homeless to find you something better than this?' I
asked.

'Why should I? It's dry and warm in winter and cool
in summer.' I was about to argue when a sharp pain shot
up from my leg and along my back making me gasp.

'What . . . what's wrong with me? What's the matter
with my leg?' I threw aside the blankets covering my
body. My legs were bound together, splints on either
side of one leg.

'You've fractured your left leg. You've been unconscious for a while but . . .'

'*What do you mean* "a while"?'

'Two days,' Phreena shrugged. 'You gave your head quite a bang when you fell.'

'Two days!' I gasped, looking at my legs again. 'Why am I not in hospital?'

'There's nothing a hospital can do for you that I can't.' Phreena smiled. 'Now . . . I've made some soup for you. I want you to drink it then go back to sleep.'

'Soup?' I frowned. 'Made from what? I'm not drinking any muck with squirrel meat or acorn pulp in it!'

'It's Campbells Oxtail actually,' Phreena replied calmly. 'I buy all my food from the shops in Callendar High Street.' I felt foolish. I drank the soup with bad grace, and without a thank you. Once I had finished, I turned to find Phreena watching me.

'I think I should be in hospital.'

'Why?'

' 'Cause I've broken my leg – what a stupid question. I don't want to stay here whilst it goes gangrenous.'

'It won't. I used to be a nurse.'

'Were you?' I asked doubtfully.

'Yes. I was. Now you'd better get some sleep.'

'I *should* be in hospital,' I argued.

'And how do you propose I get you there?' Phreena suddenly snapped back. 'Should I carry you on my back?'

'How did you get me here then?' I asked.

'With great difficulty and this cave is within a stone's throw of Betcham's Bowl.'

'You could always go for help.'

'I could do a lot of things, but what I'm going to do is something else again.'

'Why won't you help me?' Phreena and I watched each other silently.

'I am helping you,' she said at last. 'You'll just have to trust me.' I closed my eyes and fell asleep.

'When I awoke, my leg was throbbing. I opened my eyes and sat up quickly, knowing exactly where I was. There was no confusion, no disorientation, and I was strangely eager to see Phreena again. Only I saw *it* instead – the beast moving about in front of me, its shoulders stooped. Then it turned its head and saw me.

'Get away,' I shouted, terrified. I never took my eyes off it whilst my hand groped for something to throw. I got hold of my soup bowl which almost slid out of my sweaty, shaking hand and hurled it at the thing. The beast stood straight as the bowl hit it on the chest, watching me, its eyes burning into my body. I dragged myself backwards with my hands, ignoring the sharp pain spearing through my left leg with every movement. To my surprise the beast moved away from me, towards the daylight at the far end of the cave.

I breathed deeply, trying to catch my breath as I watched it leave the cave . . . but that meant nothing. It might come back at any moment! And where was Phreena? Had the beast got her? Was she dead? Torn apart? *Eaten?* Desperately I looked around for a weapon but there was nothing. My clothes, the blankets, the soup bowl . . . but that was all. There were some other things further away, like a two-ring hob and a small cupboard, but I reckoned I would never be able to make effective use of them. Not in my state. This was ridiculous. Creatures like that didn't just appear out of nowhere in Scotland in the twentieth century. But how could I disbelieve what I had seen with my own eyes?

'How are you feeling now?' Phreena walked towards me, her arms full of branches and twigs.

'Are *you* all right? Did you see it? It was just here. My God, we must do something to protect ourselves!' My words tripped over each other in my haste.

Phreena frowned. 'Are you talking about your creature again?'

'It's not *my* creature! It was here, it just left. You *must* have seen it!'

'I didn't see anything.' Phreena dropped her armful of dead wood on to another huge pile by the cave wall.

'I'm not imagining things,' I answered her unspoken question. 'It *was* in here.'

'Maybe you were asleep . . .?'

'Damn it, I was not dreaming. I saw it as plainly as . . . as I see you now.'

'If you say so,' Phreena shrugged. I was too furious to argue. I *hadn't* been dreaming. The creature had been too vivid, too immediate to be anything but real. Or I was losing my mind.

'So how are you feeling? You never answered my question.'

'All right,' I replied ungraciously. 'My leg only hurts when I breathe and my head's pounding like a pneumatic drill.'

'Do you want some aspirin?'

'I want to go to a hospital or a doctor,' I snapped.

'I've got chicken for dinner and potatoes and . . .'

'Why are you changing the subject?' I frowned. For the first time I wondered if perhaps Phreena was more than she seemed. An escaped convict? A loony? Chiding myself for an overactive imagination I watched as Phreena bustled about the cavern.

'Who are you?' It was only when she turned slowly to look at me that I realised I had spoken aloud.

'What do you think I am?' she asked without smiling.

'What do you mean? I know *what* you are. I'm wondering *who* you are.'

Phreena lowered her head.

'Don't do that,' I ordered. 'Look at me. I want to see your face.' Immediately she raised her head. She really was one of the most beautiful women I had ever seen.

'No one knows I live here,' Phreena said at last. 'That's the way I want to keep it. I have no other home, nowhere else to go, no friends . . .'

'Is that why you're keeping me here, for company?'

'Sort of.' Phreena walked over to me, knelt by my side and pulled the blankets off my legs. She stared at them for a few moments. Even in the half light of the cave her eyes seemed to become brighter, almost luminous. I admit that they intrigued me. 'Your leg is fractured, that's all. The rest of your body is fine, I promise.'

'But you can't be sure,' I said.

'Yes I can,' Phreena replied quietly. And somehow I knew she was telling the truth. When it grew dark, Phreena lit a few candles after setting up a barrier at the cave mouth.

'It keeps stray dogs and animals out,' she explained.

'It won't keep that creature out!' I muttered, but she heard me.

'Not that again,' she sighed. 'Look, I've been living here for years and I've never seen anything that looks even remotely like the thing you described.' I was too tired to argue. She talked to me about her job until I fell asleep.

Our days fell into a regular pattern after that. Phreena fed me, washed me, made me laugh, made me think. She wouldn't hear of getting a doctor for me though, instead she always unsubtly changed the subject. And after a while I stopped asking. After a little while longer, I didn't particularly care. Phreena was taking good care of me, Phreena actually cared for me. After the pounding my ex-lover Beth had given my heart and mind, Phreena was just what I needed. I began to care for Phreena. Beth wasn't forgotten, but remembering her didn't hurt so much anymore.

But there was the beast. Although I never saw IT

again I could never quite shake the feeling that it was just beyond my sight, just beyond my reach, but always watching. Phreena laughed in my face when I told her that, so I never repeated it, but I still felt it. Before long I could hobble about on the makeshift crutches that Phreena had fashioned for me out of stout, sturdy wood. We both preferred it when I leaned on her though. Then I went and spoiled it all.

Phreena was feeding me soup and we were laughing at everything and nothing. She had such a beautiful laugh, fey and infectious. I took the soup bowl out of her hands and placed it on the floor. Then I pulled her to me. And I kissed her. Honey and fireworks. Instantly I wanted more than kisses. I wanted her. And she wanted me too. I could feel it, instinctively. Suddenly she drew away from me as though my mouth had scalded her. She leapt to her feet and turned away from me.

'You can walk now,' she said quietly. 'I'll help you to the path then you'll be able to find someone to take you down to Callendar.'

'I don't want to go to Callendar,' I said, rising to my feet with the help of one of my crutches. 'I want to stay here. I want to be with you.'

'You don't know what you're saying.' She turned around suddenly and her expression was fierce, her eyes more brilliantly green than I had ever seen them. 'I want you to leave . . . *now*.'

'Phreena, I'm sorry if I offended you, or frightened you.'

'Frightened me?' she repeated. Then she laughed. I didn't like that laugh. '*Frightened me*! You don't frighten me, I frighten myself.' I grabbed her arm and pulled her to me. I just wanted to hold her, to smell her, to taste her. But Phreena pulled away so hard that I almost fell over.

'NO!' she shouted. 'Leave. Leave now before it's too late.'

'You want me,' I said stubbornly.

Phreena stared at me. 'Yes, I want you.'

'Please don't send me away. I love you Phreena.' I knew the words were true as they left my mouth. Phreena placed her hands over her ears and screamed. I backed away from the noise. Then she looked up at me, slow tears trickling into her so-sad smile.

'I love you too,' she said softly. 'But I wish I didn't. I wish you didn't love me. You shouldn't have told me you love me . . . We would have been safe if you hadn't said that.' As I watched, the whites of her eyes slowly turned green then red.

'I tried to let you go. I did try.' Her voice was tired and sad. 'I can only . . . touch, live, on that which I love, that which loves me . . .' Scales were forming on her hands.

'I do love you my darling. But now you've made me want you.' Her face was twisting, distorting.

'It was in the nature of my . . . type . . . those of my planet must love what they destroy, and destroy the ones they love. It protects us. It ensures that we will never again be dominated.' I tried to take a step back but I stumbled and fell.

'I love you my darling. You were kind to me.' The beast growled at me.

'And because I love you, you won't suffer.' It was standing over me, its scalding hot tears falling on my face. It knelt down beside me, and kissed me.

Imagination

Of course I should have suspected something from the beginning. I look back now and wonder how I could have been so blinkered, so naive. It all started three years ago. Barry and I lived in a two-bedroom, second-floor flat and lived very happily I might add. We had numerous soft toys each which we solemnly named, and we called them all 'our children'. We would say good night to each of them in turn before we went to bed and we – or at least I – really loved them. They lived in an armchair in the living-room, the smaller ones swarming all over the oldest, and the biggest one . . . a teddy bear of four feet four inches named Captain. Our smaller bedroom was a library, with four eight-feet tall bookcases, with at least six shelves in each. Barry and I were very proud of the fact that we had assembled them ourselves at a fraction of the price we would have had to pay if we had bought them already assembled.

We loved books. Neither of us could pass a book shop without entering it and we rarely came out without having bought at least two books each, and frequently it was a lot more than that. And that was why all the trouble started. After a year in the flat we could barely move for having to step over books on the floor. Before sitting down on any of our chairs we would first have to move a pile from the chair seat . . . So we decided to move to a bigger place, to accommodate all the books. We'd keep them in one room and they would live in proper bookcases and they would be catalogued like a real library. So we started viewing houses.

Barry wanted a flat but I told him there was no way we would get a flat big enough to hold us, the 'children' and the books we could afford – well, not in the area we wanted to live in anyway. He finally and reluctantly agreed that I was right when he had seen the price lists of the many estate agents we were receiving information from. At that time I was working as a computer systems programmer on a project which my boss was urging me to complete quickly. It was an important project so the pressure was coming from the top, at least that's what my boss told me. As a consequence Barry had to view a lot of houses by himself. We agreed in principle to the type of house we were looking for and decided that Barry should still view the houses even when I couldn't accompany him, but that we would make the final decision together, *before* we parted with any of our money. At least that was the theory.

I came home in a taxi after working late on February the fourteenth – I remember the date because I was looking forward to my Valentine's Day card and present – and was confronted as soon as I had shut the front door.

'I've found it,' Barry told me, a huge grin on his face. He stood in front of me in the hall, not letting me pass.

'Found what?'

'Our perfect house.'

'When? Today?'

'That's right. You're going to love it. It's about three miles from here. It's a four-bedroom, detached house with two receptions and a huge kitchen. It's got bay windows and a real garden but you can't have everything.' Barry wasn't that keen on real gardens. Real gardens meant lawns which had to be mowed, a problem we never had in a second-floor flat.

'Four bedrooms?' I frowned. 'We can't afford anything that big.'

'Yes, we can. It needs a few things doing to it which is why it's within our price range.'

'What sort of things?' I asked, suspicious of what was to come next.

'Oh, a spot of paint here and there,' Barry shrugged. Barry was *not* a DIY man. He complained if he had to open the fridge to get his own dinner.

'But I thought we'd agreed that we wouldn't buy a place where we would have to spend the next ten years decorating it,' I reminded him.

'It's not *that* bad. All it needs is a bit of paint. A couple lived there with their five children.'

'*Five children*!'

'Well, their five adopted children. Their own children are all grown up and live away from home now. The new children arrived with problems and drew on the wallpaper and peeled it off the walls and kicked the skirting boards . . .' Barry hesitated when he saw the expression of horror on my face. 'Anyway,' he continued, '. . . that's why the house is being sold so cheaply – because of one or two minor problems that we'll have to fix.'

'Paint won't fix holes and chipped wood in the skirting boards . . .'

'I've already told you Maggie that the house is in very good condition, especially considering all the things they told me. They were very honest with me and, besides, the adopted children aren't the ones causing the havoc now anyway. Its the children they foster who tend to do the damage.'

'They have foster children as well?'

'Yes, they're a very nice couple.'

I tried to visualise the house. A house which only needed a spot or two of paint according to Barry. All I could see was a house with peeling wallpaper, pen and pencil scrawls over the paintwork and chipped and dented woodwork.

'Well, I'll go and see it but it doesn't sound like the sort of house we wanted.'

'You'll love it and . . . well, I've already put a deposit on it.'

I stared at him. 'You've done what!'

'Now don't get angry. Don't worry, its returnable.'

'That's not the point.' I was furious.

'Look Maggie, a house like that would have been snapped up if I hadn't put a deposit on it first. It's a really nice house and structurally sound. It's got double glazing.'

'I don't give a toss about the double glazing! How could you put a deposit on it without letting me see it first?'

'I've already told you, it would have gone to someone else if I hadn't put down that deposit.'

'Then how come it hasn't been sold already?'

'Well, it's only been on the market for about three weeks.'

'That's long enough for a house of this quality.'

Barry frowned deeply at the sarcasm in my voice.

'Mr and Mrs Johnson said that the people who have come to see it so far have been put off by the amount of decorating that will have . . .' His lips snapped shut when he realised what he had said.

'So much for a spot or two of paint!' We had our first real quarrel then and it lasted for nine minutes and forty-one seconds. That was my St Valentine's Day present! We went to see the house together on the following night. I hated it.

It was worse than I had imagined, and what I had

imagined was bad enough. Light fittings and plug sockets were cracked and broken, nowhere was the wallpaper completely intact. Two bedrooms had so much wallpaper removed that they would need to be completely redecorated – even the ceiling had been drawn on in three of the bedrooms. The ceiling above the landing had damp patches in the Artex where the rain had come through the roof; the front reception was used as a playroom for the children and consequently looked as if it had been hit by a force-eight earthquake, and the back reception room and kitchen were filthy. The whole house made my skin crawl and I hated it. Two and a half months later we moved in.

I had told Barry my feelings about the house when we returned to our flat after my first visit. He said he loved it and I was just being difficult and selfish. We had our second quarrel then which resulted in him slamming out of the flat in a fury and me in tears. It was the first time he had done that and I felt absolutely miserable. I told myself that no house was worth all this misery and aggravation. I told myself that Barry was right, I was being selfish. I told myself that as long as I was with Barry it didn't matter where we lived and, OK, so we'd have to decorate the entire house before it was habitable, but at least we'd be together. I loved him. Barry returned after three hours and I told him that we could buy the house. I gave in.

We had been in the house – I never called it home – for exactly forty-eight hours when our next-door neighbour called in. I remember Barry and I were watching the news, (it's funny how I seem to remember these little things) and I was the one who had to go to the door when the door-bell rang, as per usual.

'Hello, I'm Jacqueline Duvall, your next-door neighbour. I just stopped by to invite you and Barry to dinner on Saturday.'

'Hi, I'm Margaret,' I told her with a grateful smile. 'Thanks for the invitation. Come inside.' I held the door open wide for her to enter.

'I can only stay a minute,' she told him as she walked into the hall. I didn't really hear her. I was too busy scrutinising her appearance. She was tall, at least five feet ten inches and the heels on the shoes she was wearing carried her up to six feet one or two. Her legs seemed to come up to her earlobes and the trousers and silk shirt she was wearing emphasised every curve, every contour. She wore her curling red hair superbly cut short, the slight curls framing her face which was lightly made-up. She was stunning . . . and I felt like a dumpling. I was five feet four inches – exactly a foot shorter than Barry. He said it made me seem more cuddly and anyway he didn't want an Amazon in his bed. I felt that if I wasn't chubby, I was at least heading in that direction.

'Who is it darling?' Barry called from the back reception room which we had decided to use as our living-room.

'It's our next-door neighbour, Jacqueline Duvall. She's come to invite us to dinner this Saturday.' Barry was in the hall before I'd finished my sentence. He smiled. She smiled. I watched.

'Jacqueline, this is my husband Bar . . . but you know his name already.' I was careful to keep my expression clear and smiling but inside I was puzzled. How had she known Barry's name . . .? He hadn't mentioned already meeting our neighbour. Telling myself not to be a suspicious biddy, I dismissed the thought from my head, convinced there was a perfectly logical explanation. It was not long coming.

'We met briefly when Barry first came to look at the house,' Jacqueline told me with a smile. 'I recognised him at once of course but he didn't recognise me. Mind you, it was a long, long time ago. We used to be in the same class at school . . .' Out of the corner of my eye, I saw Barry's almost imperceptible shake of the head . . . or had I imagined it? I must have imagined it.

'Oh,' was all I said, then I changed the subject. 'Anyway Barry, what about this Saturday? We're not doing anything . . .'

'We'd love to come Jacqueline. Thanks for the invite.' Barry spoke to her directly. I watched.

We had dinner with Jacqueline that following Saturday and by the end of the evening I hated her. She had neglected to inform us that we were to be her only guests and she spent the entire evening practically ignoring me and flirting with Barry. He loved it. When we returned home after midnight – which was almost four hours *after* I'd wanted to go home – we had our third quarrel. He told me that I was imagining things, that I was being ridiculous. I might have believed him if he hadn't then gone on to sing the praises of our neighbour . . . her wonderful cooking, her beautiful house, her sparkling wit . . . I hated her. And I . . . I thought that I was beginning – just beginning – to hate him . . .

We both took one week off to try and make the place even half-way habitable. I had to return to work after that and my late nights started almost immediately. My work, which until we had moved had caused me a great deal of satisfaction, suddenly became irksome.

I was beginning to hate something else. I would arrive home each night in the taxi my company paid for, to find the house in a mess and no food waiting for me. Quarrel followed inevitable quarrel. By now I had stopped counting them. Sometimes I would come home to be assailed by the strong smell of bouquet or lavender in the bedroom. Barry said that he had to keep the house smelling nice. When I told him I would prefer the house *looking* nice and then the smells would take care of themselves we had another quarrel. I have always loathed the smell of aerosol air-freshener. It makes my head hurt and my throat sore. Barry knew this of course, so what was I supposed to deduce when practically every other night for a couple of weeks our bedroom would stink of air-freshener. After two weeks I'd come to find the whole house smelling of it, not just the bedroom. He was doing it to upset me. I was tired. Work was getting me down, the house was depressing me, Barry's selfishness was wearing me out. I was very tired.

Barry insisted that I look after the mortgage and insurance details, not to mention the bills. I would spend my weekends – when I wasn't actually at work – sorting out what had to be paid and when. I arranged the standing orders to pay the regular bills and sent off the cheques to cover the house insurance and our life assurance. I did everything. Barry didn't lift a finger. I started smoking again. I'd take half of Barry's cigarettes out of his cigarette packet each morning and I would usually finish them before I had finished my breakfast. I began to wonder what falling out of love felt like. Was it this tired feeling? A sad, tired feeling deep in your heart? I longed for a holiday . . . for a break. I wondered if I was heading for a breakdown. Relief came from an unexpected source.

My company sent me on a course – a residential course – which meant that I would be away from the house for two weeks. I was actually looking forward to it and Barry wasn't exactly disappointed to hear that I was going either. I left on Sunday morning. Barry took me to the train station. On the way there it was almost like old times, we laughed and joked and smiled and I was suddenly sorry I was going. I was going to miss him after all.

After two and a half hours on the train and a short taxi ride, I arrived at Deynsham Hall. I had been shown to my bedroom, and had barely begun unpacking when I realised that I had forgotten the report I had been asked to prepare and bring with me. A report I had spent three weeks on, a report which was vital to the course, a course which was vital to my promotion prospects. I could have screamed.

Picking up my handbag, I marched down to the reception to order a taxi but, luckily, a taxi was just coming up the drive, dropping someone else off. I asked the taxi driver to take me back to the station and one hour later I was seated on a train taking me back home. I had given Barry a check-list, asking him to double check the contents of my holdall to ensure that I hadn't forgotten anything. The report had been at the top of my list. He hadn't even done that for me. He was in trouble! Three hours later, I was walking down my street towards my house. I was *furious*.

I was about three houses away from telling Barry exactly what I thought of him when it happened. I saw her – Jacqueline – standing at the bay window of *my* bedroom. She was looking up at the sky, her left hand holding the net curtain away from the window. I froze. Barry appeared. His arms stole slowly around her waist whilst he nibbled at her neck, making her laugh. The curtain fell back into place and they disappeared. I was trembling, shaking. I walked slowly to the front door of our house, standing before it as I stared up at our bedroom window. Our . . . Their . . . Jacqueline and Barry. In *our* house. On *our* bed?! Between *our* sheets. I must have been wildly mistaken, dreaming, imagining . . .

I walked to the front door and used my key to open the door very slowly. I could hear music – *my* tape of Mozart's Eine Kleine Nachtmusik – greeting me from upstairs as I shut the front door carefully behind me. I crept up the stairs, slowly, very slowly, the cigarette forgotten between my fingertips. At the top of the stairs I paused. Our bedroom is to the right of the stairs, with only the bedroom door visible from the landing. I could hear them. I took a quick breath, gulping down the pain inside me, gulping down her perfume, expensive, cloying, sickly-sweet . . . Her perfume. I remembered it from the first time I met her, when she had smiled and invited Barry and me to dinner. Now I knew the reason for the air-freshener.

I hated her.

I hated him.

I wanted to hit out and hurt and destroy.

I clenched my hands into fists, tears streaming down my face.

I crept back down the stairs calling myself all kinds of coward. I opened the front door, closing it quietly behind me. I walked away, my footsteps fast. I didn't turn back once.

I made my way back to Deynsham Hall.

I finished unpacking.

Every action, every gesture was automatic. All – *all* – I could think about was Barry and that woman, Jacqueline. Smiling, laughing at me, making love behind my back . . . in my bed. Why in my bed? Why not in her house? I guessed that must have been Jacqueline's idea. An extra little dig at me; a funny little joke at my expense. Barry wouldn't have thought of that. He was too much of a coward, a selfish coward. No, the joke had Jacqueline's name stamped all over it.

I found my report in my briefcase after all. I hadn't thought to look in there, I was so sure that I had put it in my holdall. I tried to force myself to think of other things but all I could hear was Barry and Jacqueline, and my imagination did the rest.

Suddenly I couldn't take any more . . . I was wound

up like a spring and just as ready to explode. I threw myself down upon the bed and stared up at the painted white ceiling. Slowly I played the whole morning through my mind, frame by frame with the ceiling as my picture screen.

I climbed the stairs listening to the music and the laughter, smelling Jacqueline's sickly-sweet perfume. I stood still at the top of the stairs, my hands clenched and burning, and moved towards the bedroom. I stood in the doorway watching Barry making love with Jacqueline. And my hands burned.

Moments later Jacqueline saw me. 'We're being observed darling,' she said calmly.

'Bitch,' I fumed silently, 'copulating bitch.'

Barry turned his head in surprise and rolled off Jacqueline as soon as he saw me. He looked stricken, horrified . . . at being caught, I guessed.

'Really Maggie,' Jacqueline smiled triumphantly. 'You might have waited until we'd finished before interrupting.'

I moved to the foot of the bed, the duvet on the floor under my feet. My fingers were splayed out, not touching each other, my hands still burning. It was as if all the hate and hurt were concentrated in each fingertip.

'What are you doing here?' Barry said furiously. 'You're supposed to be at Deynsham Hall.'

'How can you do this to me?' I silently implored. I leant over to touch him. I wanted him to hold me and tell me that my eyes had been mistaken. I wanted to touch him and never let him go. I leant further over and touched his foot which was closest to me. Barry screamed and instantly drew away.

I stared at him in surprise. What did he think I was going to do? I followed the line of his horror-stricken, pain-filled eyes. The skin was blistered and peeling where I had touched it. I stared at his foot, I stared at Barry's face.

'I didn't mean to do it,' I pleaded with my eyes, reaching out

my hand. Barry scuttled away from me, staring at me as if he'd never seen me before.

Jacqueline leapt off the bed, her expression frightened, yet determined. She picked up the chair and walked towards me. I moved backwards, stumbling a little as the duvet under my feet tripped me up. She swung the chair at me, I grabbed one of its legs. Without warning the chair blazed alight like matchwood. Jacqueline dropped it immediately, then stared. With a scream of frustration she hurled herself at me, spitting abuse, her flailing arms trying to connect with my body. I caught hold of her wrists, and jets of blue flame arrowed up her arms . . . Her hair caught fire. Then she was drenched in a shroud of dusk-blue flames, all within moments. She fell to her knees, silent now. I let go of her wrists, horrified, and watched as she fell across the doorway, her whole body ablaze. The carpet around her began to smoke. Her burning body smelt strong, pungent, almost sweet.

I looked towards Barry. He sat drawn up and cowering on the bed. I couldn't hurt him. Much as I hated him I loved him. Still defeated, I turned away, and walked through the flames of the burning carpet and duvet and stepped over the burning body of my lover's mistress, past the now blazing door. I walked through a forest of roaring spitting flames but felt no pain. I left the house, closing the front door carefully behind me and walked back to the train station, my head bowed. I sat and waited patiently for the train which would take me back to Deynsham Hall.

The images I had seen as I stared at the ceiling faded and disappeared. Exhausted, I blacked out. Later that evening I had dinner in my room after which I put the tray outside my door, cleaned my teeth and went to bed . . . crying. Goodness only knows how I managed to get through the first day. I didn't take anything in. I kept wondering what I should do. What would I do without Barry? I was ashamed of myself, the independent woman now terrified of being alone. I knew I would

101

forgive him. Maybe I wouldn't even tell him that I knew about Jacqueline.

That evening the police arrived, a man and a woman. They told me to brace myself as they had bad news for me. 'We regret to inform you that your husband Barry Sharpe was killed in a fire at your home yesterday afternoon . . .' Here the policewoman gave an embarrassed cough. '. . . A woman was also killed in the fire. We believe it was your next-door neighbour, Jacqueline Duvall . . .' I fainted. They revived me and issued immediate condolences.

'How did it happen?' *Was that really my voice?* 'How did the fire start?'

'We believe it was started by a cigarette, but we'll know more after the debris has been examined. Your husband did smoke didn't he?' I nodded.

'The fire spread pretty rapidly. They were trapped in the . . .' Another delicate cough. '. . . In the bedroom and unfortunately, the double glazing was toughened, sealed glass. Apparently your husband tried to smash the windows but he couldn't break them . . .'

The images conjured up earlier during my blackout rose once again to the surface. *But they were only images . . . weren't they?* Had . . . had I done it? I could see the fire spreading, burning ever higher, ever hotter . . . My God! Suppose the police ever found out. *But why should they?* They said a cigarette did it. I fell to my knees and wept. All I could see was Barry hammering at the double-glazed windows, shouting to be freed. Poor Barry.

The policewoman helped me to my room and then left me alone. I cried until I had no more tears left. It was strange . . . but once I had stopped crying I didn't feel tired any more.

Such are the Times

I tried not to panic, I really did. But the rain was only minutes away, I could smell it. I walked faster and then my walk broke into a run. The dying sunlight glittered through the trees like a tinkling laugh, a laugh directed at me and the futility of trying to escape the rain. The sky was more blue than white but experience had taught me that meant nothing. Here I was in a nameless winter forest with no cover in sight, and if I didn't find shelter soon I would die. And I didn't want to die.

I didn't have much – like thousands (millions perhaps) of other people left in the world. I was used to living hand to mouth, day to day. Everything I had in the world I carried in a bag on my back and it contained nothing I wasn't prepared to lose. If I were to get caught in the rain there would be no one to remember me, let alone mourn my passing. But I wasn't ready to give up yet.

So I ran, around gnarled trunks, over the concrete-hard ground, my head darting first here then there, searching for some kind of shelter. Ten minutes in the rain was enough . . . The rain was still full of the acids and pollutants created by the last war, a war with a new chemical weapon. My mother had called it the Sad War; I thought the name apt. Most of the people I met on my travels were sad – remembering how things had once been. Most people were unfriendly, belligerent even. I could understand that; in these times it was the

103

only way to survive. Such are the times we live in.

Then I saw it. A light up ahead. I pelted for it, ignoring my aching legs, the pain in my ankles. I turned my face to the sky and sniffed. The rain was closer, the sky behind the trees was rapidly turning to darker shades of grey. It was a house, more like a cottage really, with a light on in one of the ground-floor windows. I didn't care about that. It was shelter. I would take my chances with the occupants of the house. In the rain I had *no* chance.

I banged on the door, again and again. I felt a burning raindrop on my cheek. I panicked, felt for the door handle and turned it. Thank God it was open. Another scalding raindrop fell on my forehead before I stumbled across the threshold. Kicking the door shut, I leaned against it, forcing myself to calm down. I was inside now . . . safe?

'Hello, is anyone home?' There was no answer.

'Hello?' I shouted again, looking around with tired curiosity. It wasn't particularly clean. It smelt musty, uncared for . . . but it was dry and that's all I cared about. I entered the closest room, the room with the light.

'Hello,' I tried again feebly. Maybe the house was empty. I hoped so. I wanted to be alone, to relax for the first time in weeks. The occupants were probably somewhere sheltering from the rain. I wished . . . I hoped they had been caught in it, then they would die and the house would be mine. Such are the times we live in.

The room was quite large, its walls a dingy yellow-brown. What light there was came from a fireplace and two candles on a battered, three-legged stool. Against the opposite wall to the fireplace was a settee, dirty and worn, with the stuffing appearing in odd places through the cushions. But it had to be more comfortable than the hard, wood floor so I sat down after taking off my back-pack, and continued to look around. A tiny table was placed beneath the one small window to my right but apart from that the room was empty. I leaned my head back and sighed softly. I was right. The chair was soft, the fire was warm and I was out of the rain. I closed my eyes gratefully. Suddenly my head was yanked back, something sharp and cold pressed against my throat. Instantly I knew and felt that it was a knife – with a *very* sharp edge.

'Who the hell are you?'

I couldn't see the man behind me. I was too frightened to turn my head. Besides, the tiniest movement on my part and he would cut my throat, that much I did know. Hell! He might cut my throat anyway.

'Answer me,' the man demanded again. 'Who are you and what are you doing in my house?'

'I . . . my name's Bob . . . Bobby. I'm sixteen . . . It started to rain, I came in for shelter. I'm . . . I was tired. I didn't mean to trespass . . .' The knife moved fractionally away from my neck.

'I want you out of my house . . . NOW,' the man said harshly.

'But . . . but it's raining,' I protested. 'I'll die if you send me out there. Can't I just stay until it's over?'

'The rain is your problem not mine. And besides, it might last for a month or more. You're certainly not going to stay here that long.'

'I won't be here for that long,' I argued eagerly. 'It's only going to last two days, then I'll be on my way.'

'I don't want you in my house *for two minutes*! And how do you know it's only going to last for a couple of days?'

'My nose told me,' I replied reluctantly, feeling foolish. 'I can always tell when rain is coming and how long it's going to last.'

'You can't stay here . . .'

'Please . . . please . . .' I begged. 'I won't be any trouble. I can cook, clean, chop wood . . .'

'In the rain?' he said scathingly.

'I won't be any trouble,' I argued. 'Please . . .'

Silence.

'I'm going to move the knife away from your neck now but one false move and you'll be dead before you can blink.' The tip of the knife was reapplied with force to my neck. 'Do you understand?'

'I get the point,' I replied.

The knife left my throat and I heard him move from behind the settee. I slowly, carefully, raised one hand to my throat. I had a slight cut, and it hurt. Still that was better than not feeling anything at all . . . ever again that is. I remained seated as the man moved to stand before me. I recoiled deeper into the chair at the sight of him. The candles cast strange, dark shadows over his face but even in strong sunlight I would have given this man a wide berth. He was tall, at least six feet, with dark hair and hard, cold eyes. I guessed he was over thirty and under forty. His face was the meanest I had seen in a long, long time but worst of all was the deep, broad scar running from the corner of his eye to just below his lip. I glanced down at his hand which still held the knife.

'What did you mean when you said your nose told you it was going to rain?' he demanded.

'I can smell it,' I shrugged. I decided that with this man it would be prudent to keep any answers direct and to the point.

'How old did you say you were?'

'Sixteen,' I replied . . . too quickly.

His eyes narrowed. 'How old?'

'Eighteen,' I said reluctantly.

'I thought you didn't look sixteen. But isn't your voice a bit high for an eighteen-year-old?'

'I know,' I frowned. 'That's why I tell everyone I'm sixteen. I'm lucky though. My voice may not have broken yet but that's my only side-effect from the chemical fallout. I've seen people who've been a lot worse off than me.'

He continued to scrutinise me. I shifted in my chair, suddenly aware of every lump and bump in the cushion under me. 'I've travelled a lot since my mother died ... when I was nine ...' I continued, more for the sake of saying something than for any other reason. '... I've been south to Cornwall and north to Scotland and back. I don't like to stay too long in one place ...' I trailed off as he walked to the window, his eyes rarely leaving my face. I watched as he closed the inside wooden shutters.

'Now I won't get any more uninvited guests,' he said stonily.

'Er ... what's your name?' I asked. 'I've told you mine.'

'What's it to you?' he snapped. 'Anyway, you won't be staying here long enough to make use of it.'

'Well I've got to call you something whilst I'm here,' I argued. Besides I knew the rain would last five days not two, but I had sense enough to realise that if I told him the truth he'd want me to leave immediately. Two days under his roof he might tolerate, five days was asking for a bit too much. But once I'd been here two days, I could stretch it to another three.

'Carter,' he said suddenly.

'What? Your name is Carter?' I queried. 'Is that your first or last name?'

Carter strode across to where I was sitting, grabbed me by the top of my jacket and pulled me out of the chair towards him. 'Listen to me Bob. Let's get a few things straight. If you want to stay here, you'll stay out of my way and you won't talk so much ... I don't like a lot of questions either. Get it?'

107

'Got it.'

'Good.' He released me suddenly and I fell back into the chair.

'Does that mean I can stay?' I asked immediately, straightening my clothes. Silence.

'Only until the storm passes,' Carter said at last. 'But first let me see what's inside your back-pack.'

'Why?'

'Damn it! Stop answering everything I say with a question.' Without another word I reluctantly emptied my back-pack on the seat beside me. Some bunches of herbs and a pouch filled with nuts and berries fell out first, followed by a dented flask of fresh, uncontaminated water and lastly two books given to me by my mother: the Bible and a Star Trek novel.

'What are you looking for?' I frowned as Carter rifled through my belongings. 'If it's jewellery or weapons or alcohol, you're going to be disappointed.'

'I'm glad you don't carry weapons,' Carter said brusquely, 'because I don't want to have to fight off some maniac in the middle of the night with a knife in his hand.'

'You're the one who tried to slice my neck . . . remember,' I said with indignation.

'I may still do it,' Carter said belligerently. I shut up. After searching my bag he walked to the table and sat down.

He removed a small pot from the shelf behind him and, using the wooden spoon on the table before him, began to eat.

'Aren't you going to offer me any?' I wheedled. I couldn't believe that he was going to sit there with me watching and not offer me a mouthful. He glared at me before silently turning back to his food, shoving another spoonful into his mouth. Casting a filthy look in his direction, I repacked my belongings, everything except

the herbs which I munched on slowly. I watched the
steam rise from Carter's bowl. I hadn't eaten hot food in
a long time.

'Oh for goodness sake!' he snarled, retrieving another
small wooden bowl from the shelf, 'you can have some,
but only because I'm tired of you staring at me like
that.' I almost ran to the table. This man was so tetchy
he'd probably change his mind before I'd tasted a
morsel. Carter poured about four spoonfuls from his pot
into my bowl. I scrutinised the orange-green puddle
before me.

'Has this been regurgitated?' I frowned.

'If you don't bloody want it just pass it back!' Carter
snatched at my bowl, only I got to it first.

'I didn't say that I didn't want it,' I said. 'And I trust
that this is just a taster. I mean, if this soup(?) is OK, will
you give me more?' Carter stared at me, his expression
thunderous. Then unexpectedly he started laughing, a
low, reluctant, rumbling sound.

'You have more goddamn nerve than any ten people I
know,' he muttered, a smile still on his face. 'No you
can't have any more.'

'Can I have a spoon then?' I asked, after searching my
side of the table for one. Carter took a spoon from the
shelf behind him and slammed it down in front of me.

'Boy, you are turning out to be more trouble than
you're worth.'

'My name is Bobby, not boy,' I said, picking up the
spoon, and tasting the puddle in my bowl. Instantly I
started to retch. It was disgustingly foul.

'What the hell is this?' I asked angrily.

'If you don't like it just give it back,' Carter ordered.

'With pleasure!' I pushed the bowl away from me. 'I
could make better than that with one hand tied behind
my back and one eye closed.'

'Well tomorrow you'll get a chance to prove it,'

Carter replied silkily. 'If you want to stay here, you'll have to earn your keep. You said you can cook and clean, tomorrow you'll get your chance.'

'I can't do any worse than you,' I sniffed, looking around the dingy room.

'Bobby, you are *this* close . . .' Carter said softly, holding his thumb and index-finger together under my nose '. . . to getting your ass kicked out into the rain.' We watched each other for a few moments.

'Sorry.' I said. 'Sometimes I go a bit too far.'

'I'm surprised you've managed to live this long.' Carter shook his head, returning to the muck in front of him.

'So am I,' I mumbled. I turned to stare at the wooden shutters covering the window, listening to the sound of the rain beyond.

'Why did you say that?' I turned around to find that Carter was watching me curiously. I shrugged.

'I travel a lot. I told you. I've almost been caught in the rain on more than one occasion.' Again, we silently watched each other.

'I once watched someone die in the rain,' I continued quietly, turning back to the wooden shutters. 'I was in a house, full of people when the rain started. It was the only house for miles with a decent roof. A woman arrived . . . she'd been caught in it. She pleaded with us to let her in, but the man who owned the house bolted the door and stood guard over it with a knife in either hand – he wouldn't let anyone near him. She'd been out in the rain too long . . . I watched with about five others through a side window. She kept banging on the door, screaming, her skin peeling off her face, her arms . . . Then it began to peel right off, dropping with the rain . . . I watched the rain burn the flesh off her . . . It rained for a whole day. When it stopped raining all that was left of her was sludge . . .'

'She shouldn't have been stupid enough to let herself get caught in it,' Carter said harshly, picking up my bowl to finish what I hadn't started. I watched him, careful to keep any derogatory expression from appearing on my face. I could remember the women's husband, begging for her to be let in. When the woman's screams faded so did the man's pleas. Finally he fell to his knees and sobbed. I had watched his wife die . . . I watched him survive. Such are the times we live in.

I walked back to the worn settee and sat down, picking up my herbs again and munching. 'Is this where I sleep tonight?'

Carter glanced at me. 'You can sleep where you please. But I'll warn you now, I'm a very light sleeper and I *always* sleep with a knife in my hand.'

'Is that how you got the scar on your face?' I asked.

Ignoring my question he continued, 'If you try anything – anything at all – I'll slit your throat first and ask questions later.'

'Were you born anti-social, or did the war do this to you?' I asked.

'If you had any sense,' Carter said curtly, 'you would cultivate the same hard attitude. Your age might have brought you some sympathy before but now you're getting old – just like the rest of us. If you don't toughen up kid, you're going to get trampled underfoot.'

'I can take care of myself,' I told him sternly. 'The last person who thought otherwise is now dead.'

'You don't look as though you could kill a fly – if there were any left,' Carter said with disdain.

One good thing to come out of the war? I wondered. The animals alive nowadays had cultivated the same sixth sense as me when it came to the rain and they always headed for shelter hours before the rain started. But there seemed to be very few insects left – in Britain at

111

least. I watched Carter get up and walk to the door.

'I can look after myself,' I insisted. 'I'm a vindictive, vengeful person.' Carter laughed in my face.

'And very, very young.' His expression hardened. 'So stay down here if you want to get older.'

He left the room. I placed my back-pack on the floor and stretched out, switching the knife I kept in my right boot to my left boot as I decided to lie on my right side with my back against the settee. I liked to keep my knife close at hand. Carter was a morose pig, obviously not very used to company, but he didn't *look* like a murderer. I tugged at my shirt. I longed to unstrap but decided it would be too dangerous. Instead I closed my eyes – and tried to fall asleep.

'Wake up damn it!'

'Ouch!' I exclaimed angrily after another hard punch to my arm.

'What about breakfast?' Carter demanded.

'What about it?' I repeated coolly, rubbing my upper arm.

'Earn your keep!' Carter walked away from me and opened the shutters. 'And once you've made the breakfast you can clean the house.'

'And what are you going to be doing whilst I work?' I asked, irritated.

'Reading your Star Trek novel. It's been a long time since I read a proper book.'

'I don't think that's fair,' I replied.

'I don't give a damn . . . If you don't like it you can always leave. And if you don't do it, you'll be leaving anyway.' I looked out of the window at the rain.

'Well?' Carter asked when I didn't respond.

'Why do you think the rain only attacks living things?' I asked.

'Never mind the damn rain, what about breakfast?'

'Don't you have any thoughts on the subject at all?'

'None that I'm going to share with you.'

'What did you do before the war?' I asked curiously. 'You're pretty old so you must have worked at something previous to all this. Or were you unemployed? You seem well educated, in spite of your bad manners and worse habits . . .'

'All of these attempts to get out of making the breakfast aren't working,' Carter said icily. 'And I'm not going to tell you again.'

'All right, all right,' I sighed, getting up. 'I'll cook but I'm not cleaning your bloody house which was in this filthy state when I got here.'

I went into the kitchen. Carter followed me. The kitchen was cramped and smelly. It had a wood-burning stove opposite two huge water tanks which were as tall as Carter, with a diameter of at least two feet each. These tanks had a gap of about two and a half feet between them, into which a chair had been placed. The kitchen was small enough as it was, without wasting space like that, I thought. The tanks should have been placed next to each other, touching. There were various cupboards, work surfaces covered with rotting bits of food and low ends of candles, and a small sink was next to the stove. I pointed to the door on the other side of the stove.

'What's through there?' I asked.

'The toilet.'

'Where do you keep the food?' I looked askance at the cupboards. Did I really want food out of those dirty, disgusting things? Carter studied me.

'Between the two water tanks,' he said at last. I frowned as he walked over to the tanks. He moved the chair aside and lifted the filthy, patchy lino to one side. There was a trap door totally flush with the floor.

'The cellar runs beneath most of the house. That's

where I keep my food,' Carter said, his eyes burning into me. 'You can go down there and get some, but don't think of stealing anything because I'm going to check you and your bag before you leave.' I walked over to him and peered down into the inky blackness that was the cellar.

'What about some light?' I asked. Carter picked up a candle end and thrust it into my hand, then took a match out of one of his pockets and struck it against the wall before lighting the candle.

Without another word I went down into the cellar. I'd have to find a way of pocketing the candle in my hand and the bits of candle lying around in the kitchen. I kept a number of useful, useless objects in my pockets: two candle ends, matches wrapped in a tiny scrap of cellophane, a pack of well-used cards, pins, even plasters. They were all things that my mother had given me – and so far (touch wood) I had never had the need to use anything but the cards and matches. I looked around. I was surrounded by boxes upon boxes which were swallowed up by the darkness beyond the light from my candle. I'd try to pocket some food for myself before I left. Carter obviously had plenty.

'Hurry up,' he called after me. With a patient sigh, I began to search through the tins in the box nearest to me for something suitable to eat.

'Breakfast is served.' I entered the living-room, a plate in either hand. Carter was standing by the window, staring out of it. I placed the steaming plates on the table. My hands can stand really hot things . . . it's the cold they don't like. We ate breakfast in silence, although I could tell that my host was impressed, by the appreciative noises he made as he ate the corned beef hash I had prepared. I had used dried onions but that was better than no onions at all. When Carter finished he licked the plate, slamming it back down on the table afterwards. There was no 'thank you', not even a 'that was good'.

'What *did* you do before the war?' I asked, annoyed. 'Don't tell me, let me guess . . . you wrote books on social manners and etiquette.'

'That's not too far from the truth,' Carter said dryly. 'You can tidy up now,' he added quickly as if regretting the admission.

'I'm not tidying anything – I told you that before. I'm not a bloody woman!'

Carter smiled suddenly. 'Can you play chess?'

'Yes,' I said cautiously, thrown by the change of subject.

'We'll play chess instead then,' he shrugged. 'It's a long time since I had an opponent other than myself.' I could now see why the house was so dirty. The first two games lasted about thirty minutes and an hour respectively and I was thrashed both times. The third game lasted over two hours and I was still beaten. In between I made lunch, afterwards I made dinner.

And so the first day passed. I asked Carter to show me around the house but he looked at me frostily and didn't deign to answer, though he did tell me when I pestered him further that the room next to the living-room was an empty back room. The next day we played yet more chess, then draughts using the chess pieces as draughtsmen. I was actually better than him at that, so he started cheating. When it grew dark we both read for a while. Then he went upstairs and I stayed downstairs. And so the second day passed. On the morning of the third day during breakfast, Carter was obviously annoyed with me.

'I thought you said the rain would only last two days,' he accused.

I sniffed audibly. 'Another two days of rain,' I said

115

slowly. 'I'm sorry I got it wrong before but this time I'm right.'

'Hhm!' he replied sullenly. 'You'd better be.'

'How did you get that scar on your face?' I'd been dying to know that since the first time I saw it. His expression darkened faster than lightning flashes.

'You're too damned nosy,' he hissed.

'I'm interested, not nosy,' I corrected. 'You don't look like you'd let anyone close enough to do that to you. You obviously think I'm more deadly than I look because you carry at least two knives that I know about. That's why I'm interested.' Carter dropped his fork which clattered on his plate. He stared out of the window, his expression sombre and brooding.

'A woman did it,' he said at last. 'A damned woman.'

'What did you do to make her scar you?' The question was out before I could stop myself. Carter glanced at me.

'I was stupid enough to marry her,' he spat. 'No more questions.'

'Where is she now?' I asked.

'Dead.'

'Did you kill her?' I tried to keep my voice even.

'Hell! No I did not. Some Marauders got her. Now, I mean it, no more questions.'

'Is that why you hide yourself away . . . because of the Marauders? Don't you miss people, having someone to talk to?'

'No I don't. In fact just listening to you makes me grateful for the peace and quiet I get when I'm alone. I haven't talked this much in over a year.'

'Don't you like people?' I said, ignoring the acid hint.

'No I don't. I've never met anyone I liked enough to trust, especially when it comes to women. I remember two years ago when a man and woman asked for shelter out of the rain. No sooner had they set foot in my house than the woman started making a play for me. I woke up that night with the man in my room, a knife in his hand ready to separate my head from my neck. Take my advice Bobby, don't trust anyone. Everyone wants something.'

'I don't,' I shrugged, 'unless you count shelter out of the rain. I like people and a lot of people are decent, even nowadays. The only ones I would always avoid are the Marauders – but then everyone avoids them.'

'You're a fool,' Carter said with disgust. 'You won't make it to your twentieth birthday.' I shrugged again. Maybe he was right.

We played cards for the rest of the day. Carter had to be cajoled into playing as he said he didn't like them but I refused to make dinner unless he gave in. After calling me a little kid, he played. It was more fun than either of us expected. We played all the silly children's games my mother had taught me.

Over dinner Carter said speculatively, 'You're the strangest boy I've ever met. I can't make you out at all.'

'I'm not a boy, I'm a man,' I replied.

'Have you ever had sex with a woman?' he asked.

I said scornfully, 'You don't have to sleep with a woman to be a man.'

'But it helps,' Carter said. 'And you still haven't answered my question.'

'No I haven't,' I answered.

'Maybe that's what you need for your voice to break.'

'Believe me Carter,' I smiled, 'I don't think that would do much good!'

'I sometimes miss sex.' Carter stared into the rain.

'Only sometimes?' I asked with disbelief.

'Only sometimes,' he affirmed.

'Don't you miss your wife?' I asked slowly, feeling very young and *very* old.

'My wife put me off women for life,' Carter said with venom. 'She loved to humiliate me. She damn near emasculated me. She got exactly what she deserved.'

I hesitated before speaking, unusual for me. Carter was so angry, so bitter. His wife was a bitch (so he said), therefore all women must be bitches.

'Nobody deserves to be killed by Marauders,' I said quietly. 'Marauders are the scum of the earth. They've taken over where politicians have left off . . . at least that's what my mother told me.' Carter sat broodingly silent. Without warning he got up abruptly, his chair falling over behind him, and left the room. I didn't see him until dinner time and even then he didn't say a word to me. I just shrugged it off.

On the fourth day the strappings around my chest were as uncomfortable as hell. I'd attempted to take them off the previous night but Carter clumped downstairs accusing me of 'moving about'. We argued briefly until I decided that I was wasting my breath and turned my back on him in an effort to get some sleep. In the dark silence that followed I thought he'd go away and leave me in peace. We both knew I hadn't been moving about. Hell! I'd been trying to keep extra quiet to take my strappings and padding off. Then Carter asked me if I'd like a game of chess. He obviously wanted some company so I reluctantly said yes. He was right, I was far too soft.

That same afternoon I was preparing soup in the kitchen when I heard a noise outside the house. I went to the kitchen window, rubbing off the grime which had turned the pane brown and then I saw them – *two of them* – moving towards the front door. *Marauders!*

The purple and white overalls which covered their entire bodies were a terror-striking uniform. The Marauders were the only breathing things – that I knew of at any rate – that could survive the rain because of their uniform, and I'd never met anyone who knew how they did it, or where their uniforms had come from in the first place. There were always rumblings about the Marauders being someone's private army but no one knew whose, or even if the vague rumours were true. Marauders arrived without warning and left destruction and chaos in their wake. I ran for the trap door between the water tanks and let myself into the cellar, careful not to fold the lino right back so that it would flop over the door once I had closed it. The last sound I heard was banging at the door then the sound of wood splintering and I didn't wait to hear any more.

Once down in the cellar I forced myself not to panic although I thought my heart would explode out of my chest. I was terrified. I felt for the knife I always kept on me, reassured by the cool feel of it in my hand. I was armed at least. But hell! I'd never killed anyone before, at least not directly. I'd never had to, I'd lied to Carter so he wouldn't think of taking advantage of me. There was muted shouting and crashing above me. I looked up as if to see through the ceiling. Carter . . . Was he all right? Had they killed him yet? I kept thinking that I should have shouted to warn him – should have stayed with him – but if he was dead then I'd be dead too by now. What could I do that Carter couldn't? I was smaller, far weaker . . . More muted sounds. I wasn't even sure if they were voices. Now everything was quiet. In some ways that was worse than hearing noises. Looking around into the darkness I decided that the wisest thing would be to keep out of sight until the Marauders left – or came down into the cellar, whichever happened first. Slowly I felt my way along, arms outstretched, to what I thought would be the ideal spot behind two columns of boxes that I remembered. Very carefully, so as not to knock them over, I inched around them. In the space behind the boxes I could stand up straight without being seen from the cellar trap door and I had just enough room to kneel but not to sit. I felt safer, but not safe. I counted the time by listening to my heart hammer.

Did I doze off? I can't remember but I was suddenly keenly aware of the sound of the cellar door opening. The half-light created by the open door spilled just to where I was hiding. *If they came down into the cellar* . . .

'How much food do you have down there?' The Marauder's voice was harsh, rasping.

'About enough for another two to five years,' Carter replied. I pursed my lips in relief. With Carter still alive maybe I stood a chance.

'And it isn't contaminated?'

'Some of it isn't.' Carter had informed me on my first day that none of the food was contaminated. I understood why he lied.

'Bring us some food,' the same voice demanded, 'and no tricks or I'll peel your flesh myself.'

'I'd better go down with him Captain. He might have weapons stashed down there,' another voice said.

'Good idea,' the Captain agreed. 'Keypa, make sure you watch him closely until I return. I'll search the rest of the house, there may be others hiding, in spite of what this man says. Once we've eaten we'll tie him up and you can help me fix the Comm box so that we can contact the others. This building will make a good base.'

'What about him?' Keypa asked.

'What about him? He has no value except perhaps as a cook.'

'He said some of the food was contaminated.'

'He lied. If it were tainted, why would he keep it down there? I'll wait until the Chief arrives. He can decide what he wants to do with him. Until then he will serve as a cook.'

If it was down to Carter's culinary expertise to save them, I knew they didn't stand a chance. I heard footsteps moving in different directions. One set came down the cellar steps, walking in my direction, then they stopped.

'If you have any jewels hidden,' the Marauder Keypa said silkily, 'tell me where to find them and I *may* persuade the Captain to let you live.'

' "May" don't make it,' Carter said arrogantly.

' "May" is all there is. Think carefully. A chance of life against no chance at all. It seems reasonable to me.'

'That's because you're on the persuading side of that knife. Try seeing it from my position.'

More footsteps. I could see them now, to my left. Keypa had most of his back to me. Carter was just visible beyond him. I poked my head out from the side of the top box. Carter's face was bloody and bruised and swollen. An almost imperceptible start on his part told me that he had spotted me. I licked my lips, wondering what I should do next. Carter moved closer to Keypa who rapidly backed away, waving the knife in his hand. Carter stepped forward again. I shook my head frantic-ally. Once again Carter stepped forward and once again Keypa backed away in my direction. I swallowed hard, shaking my head. By now Keypa was only about two feet away from me.

'If you move again I'll kill you,' Keypa said harshly. I side-stepped the boxes and moved towards the Marauder, my teeth gritted, but Keypa heard me, or sensed me. He spun quickly but Carter was even quicker. He lunged forward, throwing an arm around Keypa's neck whilst his other hand covered the Marauder's mouth. Keypa struggled like hell.

Carter hissed at me, 'Do it, for God's sake do it. Hurry up, I can't hold him much longer.' I took a deep breath and closing my eyes, I used two hands to thrust my knife upwards into Keypa's stomach. My hands were almost instantly wet and warm. I opened my eyes and looked at them. I withdrew quickly in horror, still holding on to the knife, and looked at Keypa's face. It was contorted with surprise and pain. Still holding his hand over Keypa's mouth, Carter let him slip to the floor. I knew he was dead before he reached the ground but Carter wasn't taking any chances. He twisted the man's neck, then pulled the body to the side of the boxes where it would be unseen. He cursed when he found that Keypa, unlike most Marauders, had no gun.

'Carter, I'm going to be sick,' I whispered, my hand over my mouth.

'Not yet boy,' he hissed. 'Wait until we've killed the other one.'

We crept up the steps to the kitchen, where Carter armed himself with a knife in either hand. I had a sour taste in my mouth. I wiped my sticky hands on my jacket as we crept upstairs, keeping away from the middle of each step to avoid the creaks and groans of the wood. I'd never been upstairs but I was too frightened to be curious. The Captain was moving about in one room. Carter turned to me, pointing at himself.

'Your bedroom?' I mouthed silently. He nodded. Quickly but silently he moved to the other side of the open door. He indicated that I should go first, waving me into the room with one hand. I stared at him, shocked. I shook my head angrily, not terribly impressed with his idea of using me for bait. Carter started making threatening faces. I tiptoed into the room when the Captain had his back to me, hoping that Carter's plan was a good one. The Captain was searching through an old-fashioned chest of drawers, snorting with disgust when all he found was clothes. A floorboard creaked under my foot and I froze. Too late. The Captain turned sharply. One look at me and he rapidly reached for the gun around his waist. Something whizzed past me and then, in slow motion, I watched the Captain clutch at the knife in his chest before crashing to the ground. Carter didn't wait for me. He ran over, relieving the Captain of his gun before turning furiously back to me.

'What the hell did you think you were doing? Were you going to stand there and watch him kill you?' I didn't speak until I was sure that I wasn't going to disgrace myself by throwing up.

'Get stuffed Carter!' I snapped. Carter glared at me before smiling slowly.

'I'm glad you're on my side,' he drawled. 'Now then, and I want the truth, how much longer is this rain going to last?'

'Another twenty-four hours,' I sighed, 'then I'll be on my way.'

Silence.

'Look . . .' Carter looked uncomfortable. 'You don't have to go tomorrow. You can stay an extra few days if you like.' I looked at him gratefully.

'If you don't mind I'll take you up on that. I'd rather wait until the Marauders have moved on.'

'That's all right.' Carter's face grew hard. 'But you still sleep downstairs and no tricks. This time I'll be sleeping with a gun.'

We stripped the dead man of his overalls, and took them down into the cellar, then stripped Keypa, too.

Next day we waited for a few hours after the rain had finally stopped, then buried the bodies behind the house. By the time we had finished I was totally distressed, smelly, dirty and longing to take my damned strappings off. I hadn't dared loosen them during the previous night, fearing the arrival of more Marauders. It seemed to me that I had spent my entire time in Carter's house afraid for one reason or another. The day after the rain had stopped, Carter and I walked for over an hour to the nearest river. I didn't want to go with him but he insisted. I dreaded getting there. Carter stripped naked and jumped into the icy water.

'Come on in. The water's lovely.'

'I . . . er . . . I think one of us should be on guard in case the Marauders haven't moved on yet,' I stated.

'Good idea,' Carter called back, before swimming away from me.

I lay down on the riverbank, closing my eyes against the sunshine. I kept remembering the look on Keypa's face when I killed him . . . I must have drifted off to sleep because when I suddenly opened my eyes Carter was kneeling over me and I instinctively knew that he'd been there for a while. I stared up at him, wondering anxiously at the angry, sombre look on his face.

'Hello,' I frowned, uncertain.

Carter's breathing was deep, audible. He stood up quickly and strode away from me back to the house. Eagerly I watched him leave; now I could bathe in peace. Even my fear of the Marauders faded to insignificance against the opportunity to take my strappings off – *at last*. I took my clothes off, washed the strappings and paddings and left them on rocks on the riverbank to dry. I washed the blood off my jacket then jumped into the river, with my knife still in my hand. The water was freezing, but wonderful. Thankfully only the rain was lethal – once the rain stopped, it reverted back to so-called normal. Mother once tried to explain it to me but I hadn't really understood. It had something to do with certain chemicals in the upper atmosphere which affected the rain and which were only neutralised after a certain period of time at ground level. I reckoned that after about two or three generations of drinking this strange water, the chickens would really come home to roost! I swam to and fro, the knife between my teeth, then climbed out and dressed, restrapping my chest reluctantly and wrapping the padding around my waist. I went back to the house.

The days fell into a semi-regular pattern after that. I went to the river every morning, either making an excuse not to accompany Carter or going by myself when he didn't want to go at all (which was usually the case). I did all the cooking and Carter did what he called the cleaning, which wasn't worth much. We played cards and chess at which I got better and Carter got worse. Sometimes I would look up from the chess board to find him watching me, a strange expression on his face and his mind obviously not on the game. Such was life for about three weeks. Easy in an uneasy sort of way. My stay with Carter was close to being the longest time I had ever spent in one place.

One evening I asked him, 'Why don't you have any books of your own? The way you read and re-read my books, I would have thought you'd be surrounded by them.' I sighed inwardly as Carter's face took on the same hateful expression it always did when he was about to mention his wife.

'The back room used to be full of them, shelf after shelf of books.'

'What happened?' I asked. I'd only been in the back room once and it had been totally empty.

'My wife made a bonfire of them. I was meant to be away for two days but I came back early and caught her.'

'Why on earth did she do that?' I asked scandalised. Books in this day and age were like gold dust.

'Apparently I cared more about my books than I did about her. So she was teaching me a lesson.'

'What happened?'

'I got this scar on my face.'

'What did you do to your wife to get it?' I asked coolly. Carter smiled slowly, but did not reply.

On good days Carter would talk to me. But sometimes it was as if he couldn't bear to look at me, to be in the same room as me. He would disappear out of the house for hours, after gruffly asking me if it was going to rain. We still played chess but I never spoke during our games. Carter became furiously angry with me when I spoke too much. Only slowly did I realise just how lonely Carter really was, so lonely that he was only just beginning to realise it himself.

One evening, a few hours before the rain I could smell in the air was due, I went to the river for my last swim for the next three days. The air was fresh and clean and I felt more relaxed that I had done in a long time. Carter had disappeared to goodness knows where so I knew I could have an uninterrupted swim. But first I lay down on my favourite rock, closing my eyes and smiling. I knew I ought to be thinking about moving on but I was so tired of travelling. Hell! I was just tired! Sometimes I wondered if it was worth surviving like this, existing like this, but only sometimes. Life was special – Mum had drummed that into me and I believed it – sometimes.

I lay still for a long while, thinking of nothing in particular – in a world all of my own. The whispered sound of breathing made me open my eyes. Carter's face was only a few inches away from mine. He kissed me before I could stop him but as soon as I pushed at his shoulders he let me go.

'What the bloody hell do you think you're doing?' I was angry, incredulous. Carter kissed me! *How had he guessed*? How did he find out?

Carter ran his fingers through his hair. 'I'm sorry. I . . . hell . . .!' It was the look on his face that stopped me from leaping to my feet and running. He looked angry, but most of all disgusted . . . and not with me.

'You're . . . you're a homosexual!' I breathed with

relief. All this time I'd been safe and never knew it. The irony of my situation struck me then and I started laughing. I tilted my head back and roared with laughter. Carter sprang to his feet and after a bitter look in my direction he marched off. I stopped laughing guiltily. I wasn't laughing at him, I was laughing with relief. I shrugged. I'd explain that to Carter when I got back to the house, I decided. Maybe that was the cause of the trouble between Carter and his wife or maybe his wife had put him off women for life. No it didn't work like that – but hell! What did I know! It struck me that Carter had never told me his wife's name. I'd have to ask him when I got back.

I finished my swim and walked quickly back to the house, not bothering to strap myself. Carter was in the kitchen. It looked as though he was making dinner but it was difficult to tell because he had his back to me. If he was making dinner, then I was in trouble. Carter hadn't made any of the meals since I had arrived.

'Carter I . . .'

'Bob, I want you to leave. I want you to leave this house now,' Carter interrupted.

'But it's going to rain before morning,' I protested, aghast.

'Then the sooner you leave the sooner you'll find shelter somewhere else.' Carter still didn't face me. 'You can use one of the Marauder's suits.'

'Yeah, and if I get spotted wearing that thing by anyone who's not a Marauder I'll be torn apart, as I'm on my own. And if I get seen by Marauders, once they find out that I'm not one of them, I'll get torn apart anyway.'

'You'll just have to take your chances like everyone else,' Carter said stonily.

'Carter is this because . . .'

'No it isn't,' he denied harshly.

127

'But I understand. Really . . .'

'There's nothing to understand.' At last Carter swung around to face me, his expression furious. I smiled at him.

'You should have told me Carter,' I said lightly. 'I couldn't care less about your . . . sexual preferences . . . and if you'd told me sooner I wouldn't have had to strap down my breasts and pad out my waist. You can have no idea how uncomfortable . . .'

'You're a woman!' he said incredulously, staring at my body.

'Every cell!' I smiled again at his statement of the obvious. 'My name's Roberta, but I call myself Bobby. Before my mother died she told me that it wasn't safe to travel around alone. That's why I pretended to be a boy . . .' My voice trailed off as I watched Carter. He was rigid with fury.

'I didn't mean to deceive you,' I continued uncertainly. 'No . . . I mean, well I guess I did deceive you deliberately but only because you're a man . . . I . . .'

'You damned liar . . .' Carter roared at me.

'I never lied to you,' I said annoyed and more than a little anxious. 'You never said to me "are you a woman?" to which I replied "no"!' Carter took a step towards me. I hastily stepped backwards.

'I don't see what you're so angry about anyway,' I snapped. He was frightening me. 'Unless of course you're disappointed that I'm not a man . . .' *Mistake*! He grew even more angry at that. I stepped back again only to back into the water tank.

'Carter, for goodness sake! Don't look at me like that. I'm not your wife.' *Another mistake*.

He stood only a foot in front of me, his eyes burning into me. My heart pounded in my chest as I stared at him, desperately trying to figure out my next move. Without warning I darted to the right, hoping to run around him. That was my biggest mistake. He grabbed my arm and pulled me around to face him. Instinctively I knew I should have held my ground and tried to reason with him. He started shaking me hard, his face full of hate and fury. He wasn't Carter any more, I wasn't Bobby. He was just a furious, deceived man and I was the deceiver. His fingers were biting into my arms like raindrops.

'Carter let me go,' I tried to demand through chattering teeth. He shook me harder at that before suddenly releasing me. I fell backwards on to the hard kitchen floor, winded and hurt. Carter fell to his knees beside me and leaned over me. I thought he was going to strangle me. I battered at him wtih my fists, trying to get him to move back. He grabbed my flailing arms, pulling them above my head. He stared at me, loathing on his face. His breathing was as heavy, as ragged, as mine. Then, unexpectedly he kissed me. Hard. I could taste blood in my mouth. And then he raped me.

When he'd finished, I lay on my back staring at nothing. I heard him get up and slam out of the house. I lay still for a while, trying to distance myself from my . . . body. When at last I stood up my mind was very quiet. I was shaking and inside, deep inside, I was screaming. But my mind was quite calm and clear. I knew what I had to do. I got dressed quickly, my chest strapped and the padding back around my waist. Then I took the matches out of my pocket. I picked up my Star Trek novel and set fire to it, leaving it in the living-room. Then I went into each of the downstairs rooms and set fire to whatever would burn. I left my final match on the bottom step and walked slowly out of the house, ignoring the flames crackling all around me. I walked some yards away from the house before turning to watch it burn. The sky was now a dusky blue-black – a perfect backdrop for the conflagration.

I watched the flames grow higher and higher each moment, licking at the sky. I sniffed the air, satisfied, sad. I heard running behind but I didn't turn around. I continued to watch the house. The flames were lovely: blood-red, blood-orange, blood-yellow. The heat warmed me. I wrapped my arms around myself.

'What have you done?' Carter stood beside me, angry, incredulous . . . frightened. I didn't flinch away from him. We watched the fire together, the house a mass of flames now. It was almost impossible to discern the original structure. I sniffed again.

'It's going to rain within the next few hours – and sooner rather than later too,' I whispered.

'You . . . but we'll both die. *You'll* die.'

'And so will you,' I said bitterly, turning to face him for the first time. 'As my mother used to say to me Carter – such are the times we live in.' Then I bowed my head and cried.

The fire lasted for over an hour, crackling, then dying before our eyes, without a word passing between us. And the rain was closer. Very little of the original structure remained in place afterwards. Most of the house was razed to rubble. I turned slowly and started to walk away. I wanted to be alone when the rain started, but Carter grabbed my arm and turned me around to face him.

'Look! What do you want me to say? I'm sorry . . . more sorry . . .' I flinched and pulled away from him.

'Hell, oh Hell . . .' he said harshly. 'I . . . I don't want to die Bobby. I don't want *you* to die either and we . . . we can survive this. We can *both* survive this.' I looked up at him, saying nothing. It was strange how ghostly-silver his face looked in the fading moonlight. Gaunt and ghostly. Did I look as strange?

'If we . . . if we can clear the rubble from over the

cellar door we could stay down in the cellar until the rain stops.' Still I said nothing.

'But I can't do it without you. Hell! Even with you we might still die, but with your help maybe . . . maybe we stand a chance. You've survived this long . . . Bob . . . Bobby . . . Surely you don't want to die like this . . .'

And we watched each other – silently.

Necessary Evil

The others in this building call themselves by all sorts of fancy titles: call-girl, rent-boy, escort, gigolo . . . I prefer the more innocuous term of worker (when I'm in a good mood) or whore (when I'm not).

We're not allowed out of this building, euphemistically called the Home. We're not even allowed on the ground floor. There are gyms, swimming pools, cinemas, even a theatre in the Home, so the Authority argue that we have no need to go anywhere else. Everything we could see and do outside has been brought inside, our every wish is catered for. I don't mind not being allowed out of the building, but some of the others do. I have my dreams . . . and the roof.

The Authority regularly warns us against trying to escape. And of all the people who have tried – that I know about at least – none of them has made it to the outer door. Those who try to escape, disappear. Puoff! Here today, gone and forgotten tomorrow. Would-be escapees are known in the Home as shadows in the dark. Within hours of the failed escape attempt (and they would always fail), the dead (and they would always die) had their rooms redecorated, and all record of them vanished. It would be as though they'd never existed. There were no funerals, no remembrance services for any who died, regardless of the cause. We provided an unwelcome but necessary service and as such were treated as a necessary evil.

The Home was twenty-five storeys high – each storey had twenty apartments, ten on each side of the main corridors. There were lifts at both ends of the corridors and a staircase which ran down the middle of the building, reached via double doors in the middle of each corridor. As we were not allowed to leave the building I occasionally wondered what would happen if there was a fire or an earthquake. Would the Authority relax its rules then? Somehow I doubted it. We each had our own apartment which was our only responsibility. Our clients were always entertained in those apartments, which consisted of a bedroom (naturally) for the old-fashioned kind, a kitchen, living quarters and a Play room. Of course, most of my clients preferred the Play room. All they had to do was drink the MindBender and zoom! Instant mental teleportation to anywhere in the galaxy.

Anywhere, that is, within the client's conscious mind as the client would have to make a conscious decision to go there. New sights, new settings, make-believe worlds in far-away places. And they took me with them. The Play room disappeared to be replaced by the sounds and smells and feel of the new image. I loved the sea scenes best. A crashing, hostile sea with the spray splashing my face and the waves roaring at me. I liked mid-grey skies and darker grey oceans and the tang of salt and the soft crunch of the sand beneath my feet. I could stand for hours hand in hand with a client as we drank in the scene together.

Some of my clients were weird though. The weirdies projected us to dark places, dangerous places. They liked the idea of me as a woman in dire distress, in need of rescuing. Some of the creatures they conjured up were quite obscene. I had one client, Mr Stugins, who visited me twice a year. I dreaded seeing him, his mind was evil. No one was ever supposed to get hurt during a mind projection but sometimes with him we would come close – too close. Mind projections were supposed to be like dreams or controlled nightmares where the client could pull out, 'wake up' just in time. Mr Stugins found it exciting to come as close to dying as possible. He gave me the creeps. I tried to get him switched to another worker but he was obviously someone very influential because the Authority refused adamantly and the Authority rarely intervened in requests for client transfers. My favourite client though was Mr Jones who visited me once every three months. He let me call him Sam, which wasn't really allowed but it was our little secret. He treated me like a . . . a lover. Someone special. He was my favourite.

I didn't do women or sados. My clients were *my* choice and I would only do men. Tiernan, my next-door neighbour, thought I was crazy but as I said to him, what would I use the extra money for? I couldn't even use the Play room. Workers were strictly forbidden to enter the room alone. That was the Authority's number one rule.

But the life I lived never used to trouble me. It never used to touch me. Mostly I kept myself to myself, apart from when I entertained a client or some friends. I had very few friends and that was the way I liked it. It wasn't that I loved the Authority, it was just that my philosophy was 'anything for a quiet life'. But then something happened to change all that.

Gardina, the best friend I had in the Home, tried to escape. I heard the alarm bell sound throughout the building whilst waiting for my next client, but never dreamt that Gardina was the cause of the commotion. I hated that bell. It rang in my nightmares. Tiernan reckoned that Gardina had had enough of this place and was committing certain suicide. Well I don't think she was trying to escape . . . nor do I believe that she was tired of living. Gardina felt as I did about the Home. Many times we would spend our relief hours laughing, talking, joking together – about our clients, the Home, our lives. No, she didn't commit suicide. I was convinced that she was murdered. Of course I kept that view to myself. I didn't even tell Tiernan of my suspicions. Gardina was murdered . . . but what could I do about it? Part of me didn't want to get involved and yet Gardina was my friend.

A week after Gardina's death there came a soft yet insistent knock at my door. I awoke immediately, annoyed because I'd only just got rid of my last client and dropped off to sleep. Thinking that it was another client at the door, I put on Wednesday's diaphanous negligée before calling out 'Come in'. It was only Tiernan. That made me even more cross.

'What do you want? I was asleep,' I snapped, hoping he wouldn't stay too long. Tiernan sat down on the edge of my bed, his eyes never leaving my face.

'What is it Tiernan?' I questioned after a pause.

'What do you think about . . . Gardina's death?'

'I don't want to talk about that.' I sat down beside him wearily.

'You must. I . . . tell me what you think . . .'

'I think you're bloody inconsiderate to disturb me when I should be getting some sleep. That's what I think.'

'Shut up and listen,' Tiernan snapped so suddenly that I jumped. 'What if I were to tell you that Gardina *did* commit suicide? And what if I were to tell you why?'

'Stop being so tantalising,' I snapped back. 'If you have something to say just spit it out.'

'Put on something more substantial and I'll prove what I just said. We have to use the Play room . . .'

'But it's forbidden for us to enter the Play room without clients,' I reminded him.

'I live here too remember,' Tiernan replied, 'you don't have to tell me the rules.' I stared at him. This was Tiernan as I had never seen him before and I wasn't sure how to behave with the new Tiernan.

'Gardina and I used the Play room on the day before she died.' Tiernan watched me intently. 'The day before she committed suicide.' I got dressed.

'What happens now?' I asked as we entered the Play room together.

'Take this.' Tiernan handed me a MindBender. I protested but I still took it, watching as Tiernan did the same.

'I've never had to project myself into my own fantasy before,' I said.

'We won't be projecting into a fantasy. We're going to visit the birthplace of the workers.'

'Pardon?' I said, sure I must have misheard him.

'Aren't you curious to see where you came from?'

'I know that already,' I laughed. 'I came from the same place everyone else comes from. With a few minor modifications.'

'Like what?' Tiernan's expression was derogatory, pitying. It irritated me.

'My mother gave me to the Authority when I was born because she couldn't look after me. I was never fostered or adopted so the Authority decided that the Home was the best place for me. So here I am. Simple and straightforward.'

'If that's what you believe then I think you'd better prepare yourself for a big shock,' Tiernan said grimly. 'You're finally about to discover reality.'

'But the screen projects fantasy, not reality,' I protested.

'It does both,' Tiernan argued. 'Only why would any of our customers want reality? Fantasy is much easier, so much more interesting. They can get reality outside, we can't. That's why the Authority banned us workers from using the screen. Our clients want fantasy, we want reality. The screen is just an amplifier, high-lighting whatever is directed at it.' I turned to stare at the screen then back at Tiernan. He was frightening me.

'Try to remember yourself as a child . . . no more than a baby.' I did try, I tried hard. But my mind was blank. There was nothing there, not even emptiness.

'I can't remember myself as a child.' I admitted what I had previously never even admitted to myself.

'That's because you never were one. None of us were.'

'What are you talking about?'

'What's your memory like? Good? Average? Fair?'

'Good. Very good,' I answered.

'When did you come to the Home?'

'Eight years, seven months and fifteen days ago if you want me to be exact.'

'Then think back to eight years, seven months and *sixteen* days ago.' The screen before us began to flicker. Hazy lines became more sharply defined as my memory took over. I saw a huge hall, split by partitions into sections. There were many people everywhere, all moving purposefully around me. I was there, actually *with* them, just as I was a real part of my clients' fantasy landscapes. I saw tables covered in indiscernible metal sculptures, huge rolls of fabric attached to the partitions – rolls of different colours ranging from blue-black to milk-white. Then I realised that what I had thought were rolls of fabric where in fact rolls of skin. I jumped as a woman in grey overalls and a surgical mask held up a head mould. My head . . . with no eyes. I closed my eyes as my stomach heaved. I was sick, wretchedly, painfully sick. When I opened my eyes again I was back in the Play room with Tiernan watching me. My vomit lay in a puddle at my feet and over my shoes.

'Was that true?' I whispered.

'Yes,' Tiernan replied immediately. 'Every second of it was the truth. You were made by the Authority, for use in the Home. I've already seen myself being manufactured.'

'That wasn't . . . it couldn't have been me,' I protested. 'I'm human. I'm flesh and blood.' How could I be a robot with no mind, no consciousness except that which had been given to me? Every thought, every mind pulse was my own – private, unique. How could it be otherwise?

'It's the truth,' Tiernan replied to my unspoken words.

'I don't believe it,' I said angrily. 'I don't care what's on the screen. I don't care if it *is* from my own mind. That's not me there. I can reason. I can think, feel for myself. I bleed, I hurt, *I have feelings*.'

'A credit to the Authority's manufacturing. Don't you think that I've been through all this before? Everything you're thinking now, I've thought. Everything you're feeling, I've felt. Now I've accepted the fact that I'm a robot. Gardina couldn't . . .'

'You're lying,' I screamed at him. 'I'm human, down to my bones and my soul.' I turned back to the screen. Instantly an image appeared of a man and a woman each fitting brown eyes to the mould of my face, fitting *my* eyes into *my* face. I dismissed the image from my mind and it disappeared from the screen. Tiernan placed a placating hand on my arm.

'Believe me Raina, I know how you feel but you must think about this logically . . .' I was amazed and disgusted.

'Think about it logically . . .' I repeated contemptuously. 'Think about what? Are you really going to accept that you're a robot, without questions, without a fight?'

'A fight? Raina, we're not even supposed to be using the Play room. What do you think would happen if the Authority found out that we know what's really going on? We'd be disposed of before we had time to blink. What do you think happened to all those so-called escapees? Most of them weren't trying to escape. Most of them were poor fools who'd used the Play room, found out the truth about themselves and were then stupid enough to confront the Authority with what they knew.'

'So you really do believe that you're a robot?'

'Don't you?'

'No I don't,' I replied stubbornly. Tiernan sighed then attempted a smile.

'It makes sense in a perverted way. Robots can be created so that diseases aren't transmitted. In fact we might even be killing the diseases at source.'

'That's disgusting.'

'No more so than what the Authority is doing to us,' Tiernan snapped. 'Stop living in a dream world. You'll have to face up to what's going on sooner or later.' Then Tiernan turned around and marched out of the room. I cleaned up the mess in the Play room and went to bed.

'This is ridiculous Raina. You haven't seen any of your clients in close to a week.'

'I'm ill.'

'Of course you're not ill,' the Supervisor snapped at me.

'I *am* ill. I don't feel well . . .' The Supervisor's face was puce with exasperation.

'Raina you are not ill. It's not possible.'

'Why isn't it possible?' I asked softly. His mouth opened, then clamped silently shut.

'I'm ill and I'm tired. Please leave me alone.' I turned my head away from the Supervisor and his guards. I heard them leave but did not turn around. Almost immediately I heard the door open again.

'Leave me alone,' I pleaded.

'Raina it's me.' I turned my head, then sat up at the sound of Tiernan's voice.

'Hello stranger.' I smiled. He looked sad.

'Are you still angry with me?'

'I was never angry with you,' I replied.

'I thought you were because I showed you . . .'

'You didn't show me anything that I didn't already know for myself,' I interrupted, placing a warning finger over my lips. 'I feel so weak and giddy Tiernan. Help me to the bathroom.'

Tiernan frowned as he came towards me. He helped me out of the bed and I leaned on him heavily as we walked out of the bedroom and into the living-room. He opened his mouth to speak but I shook my head, steering us towards the Play room.

'You might as well come into the bathroom with me,' I said deliberately. 'I haven't got anything that you haven't already seen.' Then we went into the Play room and Tiernan shut the door quietly behind us. Immediately I stood up straight and moved away from Tiernan.

'What was that about?' Tiernan asked.

'I think . . . I *know* they're monitoring me. This is the only room we can talk freely in. They can't bug this room because of the Sexual Privacy Act.' Tiernan and I watched each other. The wariness in his eyes was mirrored in my own.

'So you're all right? There's nothing wrong with you?'

'Nothing physical,' I replied. Taking my courage in both hands I said, 'Tiernan . . . I'm going to leave this place. I'm going to escape. Come with me?'

'To where?' Tiernan said immediately, angry. It wasn't the first question I would have asked. 'Hell, it doesn't matter where – we'd never make it to the front entrance.'

'Yes we will. I have a plan.' Tiernan was breathing hard and fast. I knew I was frightening him.

'What sort of plan?' Tiernan asked.

'Will you come with me?'

'Tell me the plan first.'

'No, it won't work if I tell you first. In fact I don't want to tell you at all, but I do have a way out of here. All you have to do is trust me.'

'Why are you suddenly so keen to leave here?' Tiernan asked suspiciously. I didn't blame him for questioning my motives. 'You're the one who loved it here . . .' I held up my hand to interrupt him.

'I never *loved* it here,' I said quietly. 'I accepted it as someone who knows their time for freedom will come. Well my time has arrived.' Silence.

'Are you coming with me or do I go alone?'

'Do you really have a way to get us out of this dung heap in one piece?' Tiernan asked. I could read all the doubts and worries and fears and hopes flickering in his grey eyes.

'I do. I promise.'

'Then I'll come with you,' Tiernan sighed.

'Thanks Tiernan,' I said gratefully. 'We'll leave tonight.'

'Tonight?' Tiernan said aghast. 'You mean *tonight* tonight?!'

'Tonight,' I repeated.

That night when Tiernan was between clients, so-to-speak, I knocked on his door.

'Are you ready?' I asked when he appeared.

'I'm not too sure about this.'

'You've changed your mind then?'

'No,' Tiernan said at last. 'I'll come with you.'

'Get dressed then.'

'What's wrong with what I'm wearing?' We both looked at his white, tight trousers and light-blue sleeveless T-shirt.

'I'll get changed,' Tiernan said ruefully. He reappeared within moments dressed all in black, as I was. In silence he followed me to the lift. We entered and I punched the button to go to the roof.

'What are you doing?' Tiernan frowned. 'I thought we were going to the ground floor.'

'Not unless you want to get blasted,' I replied. 'Credit me with better planning skills than that.'

'Why are we going to the roof?' Tiernan's frown deepened.

'Because that's our way out.' Tiernan looked at me but said nothing.

When we reached the roof, we walked in silence to the edge of the building. It was only when I stood up on the short wall skirting the edge of the building that Tiernan spoke.

'What the hell do you think you're doing? Is this your plan? Is this your way out?'

'Stand up on the wall next to me,' I said quietly. 'I want to show you something.'

'What?'

'Stand beside me and you'll see it,' I said.

Cautiously, unhappily, Tiernan climbed up on to the wall and stood beside me.

'This is . . . *was* my favourite place,' I told him as we looked out over the city lights. 'There are no guards up here because they think that the only way out from here is down.'

'And isn't it?' Tiernan asked.

I shook my head slowly.

'I used to come up here and imagine myself as one of them,' my arm swept outwards in an arc. 'One of the ordinary, boring people. Free to be whatever they choose, free to go wherever they want. I fantasised about becoming one of them some day. I would grow old with dignity, away from this place.'

'What's your plan?' Tiernan said impatiently. 'Is someone going to pick us up from here? Has one of your clients got a Flyer? Which one?'

'Gardina really was trying to escape when she died wasn't she? She didn't commit suicide.'

'Yes she did, of course she did.'

'No,' I said firmly. '*She was trying to escape*. What she didn't know was that by telling you of her plans she was committing suicide.'

'What are you talking about?'

'You're a spy for the Authority aren't you?'

'Are you mad? I hate this place as much as you do.'

'But your way of dealing with that hate is slightly different to mine.' I was still looking out over the city. I had never seen anything so beautiful. 'You betray your friends. What does the Authority give you for it?'

'I don't know what you're talking about.'

'Are you carrying a monitoring device at the moment?'

'No I am not – you can search me if you like.'

'I won't search you,' I smiled, 'you wouldn't make the offer if you were carrying something.'

'This is absurd,' Tiernan snapped. 'Do you have an escape plan or not?'

'We're both free Tiernan, in our dreams. Dreams are *all* we have. Dreams keep us going.' I pushed Tiernan off the wall, screaming as he plunged downwards.

'You won't destroy anyone else's dreams. That's for taking the only thing I had of my own away from me. That's for taking away the only thing any of us had.'

I went back to my apartment.

I never went to the roof again.

Mother in Rebellion

She considered herself to be a very good mother – the best mother. But the best mother had had enough. Her children were always fighting each other, even fighting themselves, hurting themselves. Hurting her. Sometimes if she'd had a bad year or decade or century she would lose her temper and remind her children just how much they owed to her patience. Sometimes – more often than not nowadays – her children would deliberately provoke her and even take malicious delight in doing so, even though they feared her anger, dreaded her loss of control. Sometimes she was simply too tired and would let her children get on with it with minimum intervention. The time came when the children were constantly and consistently bashing the hell out of each other. Not just day after day but year after year and decade after decade.

'My last brood might have been big and unwieldly and stupid,' she thought angrily, 'but this lot are far worse. They have intelligence and misuse it. They have understanding and choose to disregard it. I think I'll get rid of this lot (much as I love them) and start again.' (Sigh!) 'I've started again so many times. You'd think just once I'd get it right.'

So she remained silent as her children killed each other off, and those that were left she destroyed naturally by refusing to feed or support them.

'I'll have a well-deserved rest,' she thought wearily,

when she was once again all alone. 'Yes, I'll have a nice long rest. Then I'll start again in a few million years. Maybe my next brood will be better.' And she fell asleep.

Chase

He won't leave me alone. He chases me like the devil himself. I try to hide. I try to stay away from him but it gets more and more difficult . . . because I keep giving myself away. I can't help it. How can someone like me disguise herself? I deliver messages. It's all I do, it's all I know how to do. And each time my message is delivered, the same thing happens – he moves a step closer to me. I try to cover my tracks but it's no good. He always finds me. No matter how careful I am, no matter how quickly I move on, I always leave some trace behind me, some kind of clue or trail for him to follow.

I'm so tired. I don't know how much more of this I can take. How much longer can I keep running, hiding?

We met many years ago. I remember the first time I saw him. He was with the woman for whom I had brought my message. It was only when my message was delivered that I looked at him, *really* looked at him. I'd never seen anyone like him. Blue-black hair and the gentlest, saddest brown eyes. I melted. We spent one day and one night together, something I had *never* done before. I fell in love . . . for the first time . . . for the last time. And he fell in love with me. I could see it in his eyes and his mind and his heart. I didn't try to learn anything about him, I just accepted him as he was. That was my mistake. I should have learnt just how tenacious he was. I pretended we were a normal couple. But deep down I knew I couldn't stay. I warned him as we ate dinner together that I couldn't stay in one place but he just laughed, so sure of my love for him. When I moved on I didn't take him with me.

That's what he can't accept. He doesn't realise that I *couldn't* stay any longer. And that I loved him too much to take him with me. I had to go. Too many voices were calling to me, too many figures were tugging at me. I was wanted, *needed* elsewhere.

I stole out of his arms and out of his house just before dawn, never thinking he'd try to find me again. He should have been glad he'd escaped. I thought he'd chalk us up to experience. A wonderful day, a breath-taking night. I hoped he'd want to head in the opposite direction. I was . . . anxious about what he might do if he found me again. I convinced myself that our paths would never re-cross. Over and out. Onwards and upwards. But I was wrong.

It took a while before I knew for sure that he was following me. I travel fast and light. It took some time for me to realise that I – the pursuer – was being pursued. How laughable! At first I treated it as a joke. Me, *me* being chased! But the joke faded and died until I became afraid, afraid of *him*. It got so bad that I grew to sense him, almost smell him when he was close by – in the same building, the same town, the same country. I fled before him. A dead leaf caught in a windstorm, for once not of my own making.

So here I am now, standing by my bed. And he is outside my door . . . My fingers tingle and burn, my mouth dry with dread. I can hear him breathe, in-out, in-out, steady and sure. He wants me. He wants me as much as I *don't* want him. He wants me, and I'm terrified. The door opens. I can't move. I see him, for the first time in a long, long time. I'm choking at the sight of him. I still feel the same way. He means as much to me now as he did when I first saw him but I don't want him to come any closer.

'Please, *please*, go away. *I don't want you.* Don't you understand?'

Slowly he walks towards me, each step measured. He is smiling, with his lips, but most of all with his eyes. He's happy. I can feel his wonder at this feeling of happiness which has eluded him for so long. I back away but bump into the side of my bed. I don't have the strength to fight him, I don't have the strength to run – not any longer.

He breathes my name. I sigh deeply and open my arms. He walks into my embrace and my arms fold gently around him like a cloak. He kisses me, and breathes my name one last time. 'Death . . .' he whispers. And smiles as he dies.